Dear Mr. Dan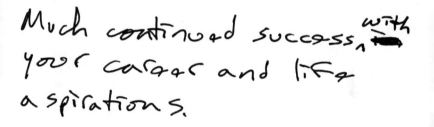 **W9-CFC-203** s,

It has been a pleasure working with you in "The Great Debaters".

From what I've witnessed, you are certainly a great talent.

Much continued success, <u>with</u> your career and life aspirations.

Hope we cross professional paths again real soon.

Best Wishes,

*(Dunbar Reed)*

June 5th, 2007

a robert x. golphin novel

# ABANDONING ADAM

*Confessions of an HBCU Scholar*

by
ROBERT X. GOLPHIN

Bloomington, IN     authorHOUSE®     Milton Keynes, UK

*AuthorHouse™*
*1663 Liberty Drive, Suite 200*
*Bloomington, IN 47403*
*www.authorhouse.com*
*Phone: 1-800-839-8640*

*AuthorHouse™ UK Ltd.*
*500 Avebury Boulevard*
*Central Milton Keynes, MK9 2BE*
*www.authorhouse.co.uk*
*Phone: 08001974150*

*First published by AuthorHouse 8/31/2006*

*ISBN: 1-4259-6025-1 (sc)*

*Library of Congress Control Number: 2006907837*

*Printed in the United States of America*
*Bloomington, Indiana*

*This book is printed on acid-free paper.*

# TEASER

HE STARED AT ME. Striking light green eyes that were deep enough to swim in. Curly dark hair and caramel skin. Clean cut. Shaven and boyishly handsome. Tall and slim like a string bean. Though his face was handsome, it was still stained with the piercing frown of disdain and confusion. His eyes really were the windows to his soul. And his eyes were lost, angry and torn. His curls were drenched in the perspiration of battle. The confliction of his mind beamed like the headlights of an oncoming vehicle on a dark South Carolina back road. He needed help. He needed allies. He needed resolution. An end to the madness of unnecessary politics was warranted without delay.

But it seemed as if no one was responding to the 'Bat-Signal' shining down on the perilous city. It seemed that everyone was afraid, or disinterested in bringing about any change in the cuckoo's nest called life. He was disowned, dissed and disrespected by many. Some even feared him. Everyone had abandoned him. But I couldn't abandon Adam. Because you see, the person that was staring at me was the reflection I saw while leaning into my mirror.

-Abandoning Adam:

Confessions of an HBCU scholar

a robert x. golphin novel

# DEDICATION

(in random order)

1. To all the **young people** within the HBCU system, or those who are considering it.

2. To my fellow soldiers:
**Lenora Jones, A.T. Miller** and **Davis Northern**.

3. To my mother, **Gail Y. Bennett**,
for raising me to question, challenge and think outside the box.

4. To my aunt, **Linda B. DesBoine**,
for teaching me to fight for that which I believe.

5. To **Zoe K. Lynch**,
for being that special someone.

6. To **Kaelyn C. Lynch**
for being a supportive and adorable lil' sis.

7. To my brother, **Christopher L. Brooks,**
for his invaluable encouragement.

8. To my grandmother, **Henrietta P. Bennett**
for making this happen!

## IN MEMORY OF:

1. My grandfather, **Jonathan Bennett,**
whose smiles about my successes lit up a room.

2. My friend, **Brian L. Jones,**
who remains my angelic partner in crime.

# ACKNOWLEDGEMENTS

(in random order)

MY LOVED ONES:

**Mary Golphin, Jacqueline Bennett, Karen & Eric Lynch, Julian R. Thomas, Antonio DesBoine & Family, The Brooks-McKnight Family,** and **Festus Farmer.**

MY HIGH SCHOOL EDUCATORS:

My English teachers, **Lorraine Sylva** and **Lois Rudman.** My film teacher, **Francis J. Radano.**

MY COLLEGE EDUCATORS:

Ella Ree Sherrod, Dr. Brenda J. Faison, Dr. Floyd Ogburn, Maria Lundberg,
Dr. Ronald L. Poulson and Janet T. Gustafson.

MY INSPIRATIONS:

NAACP President J. Whyatt Mondesire (Phila), Sonny L. Driver, Wanda Mason, Adrienne Bellamy and Elohim.

SPECIAL THANKS TO:

Robert Mendelsohn, Rel J. Dowdell, Mike Dennis, Arlene Edmonds, Scott Van Thorn, Maurice Fortune, James DiFonzo, Mike Lemon, Robert J. Clark Jr., Cinekyd, Larry Smallwood, Donna Murphy, David Morse, Matt, Linda, & Arnold Borish, Nan Bernstein, Robert Walters, and all my friends at The Greater Philadelphia Film Office (GPFO).

# PROLOGUE

WE DON'T GIVE A damn about anything! Our playground is the street. Our swing set is hip-hop. Our merry-go-round is acid. Our seesaw is fast Benjamins. Our sliding board is a fast ride. Our basketball court is a fast female. The most important thing in our lives is the kind of kicks we've got on, or what color our clothes are. What the hell do we need a higher education for? What's that going to do for us? That's not the real world. Survival in our environment is contingent upon whether we're the fittest. No textbook is going to make that happen for me. No professor is going to put that pistol in my hand so I can protect myself. No campus life is going to contribute to me being able to associate with society. Society is dangerous, potentially lethal. Attempting to reason with society is next to impossible.

Society will stab you in the heart or cap you in the dome, unless you get to it first. The society I have to interact with is far from gullible. It won't give into my efforts to feed it publicist type psycho-babble. This society and myself are walking across a wobbly eighty-foot tightrope. Both of us can't hold out forever. One of us is eventually going to fall, and fall hard. Only one of us can land on the enormous security mattress waiting below, if there should be a nasty spill. And chances are: society being as it is, will be the entity that prevails. There's no way to escape the confines of society. We've got to face it, or else.

We black folk don't go to college. And for those of us who do, we don't complete it. We come to school lacking what it takes. We don't know how to adequately study. We don't know how to prepare for higher education. And we men are the absolute worst. The sistas at Spelman College have like the highest graduation rate percentage within the entire historically black colleges and universities system. We're allowing our women to outdo us, outlive us and surpass us momentously.

We don't care how we talk. We don't care how we dress. We don't care how we smell. Courtesy for others is the furthest thing from our minds. Respect for others and ourselves is non-existent. We recognize when change is needed. But we feel that the end won't justify the means. And frequently our boxing gloves are secured solely for publicity propaganda. It matters not if we raise our voices for a purpose. Our main goal is to bathe in the shower of limelight. We wish to stand out, but only for that reason. To stand out and nothing more. Why, you inquire?

Think about it. It seems that we can't hold the office of SGA president. We aren't fortunate enough to be prodigies. And we aren't athletic superstars in the making. So standing out in any manner is a success for us. And speaking of athletics: reality dictates that if a sport is our trade, our college education is paid for in 1-2-3. But for those of us who aren't necessarily 'gifted', perhaps a 'regular' life will suit us just perfectly.

Now, I'm sure you've heard these arguments time and time again. Even if you care not to admit it. Not everyone is blessed with perfection. And though I am very conflicted as to what I should do now that the end of high school is imminent, I'll have to think long and hard before I claim one of those excuses as my own. Because there's something about earning a higher education, especially at an historically black institution, that I understand far better than some of my societal counterparts.

We're privileged to live in an era and in a country where choice and opportunity are precious privileges as well as rare gems. Our opportunity to attend an historically black college or university is both that precious privilege and rare gem. As students attending an historically black university in a post Civil Rights Era, we know that we're exceedingly blessed, and that with that wonderful blessing comes responsibility. At a time in America's history when black people can pursue higher education at any institution in the country and almost anywhere in the world, those of us privileged enough to learn, grow and develop the skills we'll need to successfully navigate the professional world at a black institution, are exceedingly grateful.

We'll always, always have that very special camaraderie that can only be attained by attending and experiencing a unique and culturally enriched black institution. I'm certain that all of us will emerge more enlightened and enriched, enabling us to carry out the mission of a fine HBCU and our own dreams, and those of our parents, and hopes for a beautiful and successful future.

But let me stress: an institution is just an institution. An administration is just an administration. Contrary to popular belief, they're not one in the same. And humans are just humans. Some of us are wise and sensible. Others of us are…well…not. And if the credibility, legitimacy and level of our higher education is compromised in any way by those who are supposed to be molding us, we not only have the right, but it is our responsibility to stand up for that which we believe.

I believe that simply allowing situations to be as they are, and not at least attempting to alter the negative states of such, is a flagrant display of lack of common sense and irresponsibility on our parts as members of the minority population. It is important and extremely beneficial for a war to be fought with an army versus that of just a lone troop. But I cannot and therefore will not try to coerce others (meaning you), into engaging in battle with me against the injustices that many times plague the higher education system. That choice is entirely up to you.

But it's with the utmost strength and respect that I encourage you to fight if you deem it proper. I also encourage that you do what my mother raised me to do. Challenge, question and never back down. Life's hardly a walk in the park. But it isn't rocket science either. You learn to ride a bike, and you fall off and scrape your knees. But when you're injured, you don't just get up and run off in tears, right? No. You get back up on the bike, and ride off into the sunset. Or at least ride, fall, ride, fall, ride, fall and continue to dust yourself off and try again. The moral of the story is, you can't just give up. If you choose to give up, then shame on you.

I'm not a rabble-rouser. I'm not a troublemaker. I'm not a militant. I'm not 'an angry black man'. I'm just a man who believes in equality, education, the past, the present and most importantly, the future.

My name is Adam S. Hinson, and I am an HBCU scholar. These are my confessions.

———◆◆◆———

# CHAPTER 1

# "A MAN'S GOTTA DO WHAT A MAN'S GOTTA DO"

'THE PHILADELPHIA INQUIRER'. THAT was my first taste of literacy. I was about 3 years old. And already I was trying to read the newspaper. Of course I had the paper upside down. But what the world deemed as just cute toddler behavior, fate determined as the precursor to something bigger. It was destiny that at such a young age my mind would already be forming ideas, and that I would take an interest in something other than the big yellow bird and his fluffy brown pal on the television screen. I was eager to learn, and learn and learn some more. And for years that's exactly what I did. It didn't take long before I jumped on the opposite side of the fence. Instead of reading newspapers and books, I myself began to write.

I concocted crazy fantasy stories about castles and kings, princesses and fire breathing dragons and somehow always managed to fit my family members into these stories. And my teachers would always give me gold stars and check marks because I finished my work successfully. But no one really ever nurtured my writing talent. No one that is, except for my mom. But I wasn't your typical average kid. I was wise beyond my years. I think I was born different. My mother has been telling me for years that when I was a baby and didn't want to be bothered with certain people who had a fetish for picking me up and cradling me in their arms, I'd just pretend to be asleep. And as soon as the unwanted guest would depart, I'd awaken with a grin on my face. I was smart. And I knew even then that it was a mom's job to say: 'Well done.' or 'Great job!'. But I needed the validation from someone else. That's what I thought my teachers were supposed to be giving me. But they never did.

In the long run, I guess it didn't matter. Maybe I didn't need anyone to tell me that I was good at being creative. Maybe it was my job to deem myself 'a creative genius'. Because years later when I matured into a teenager, it was then that my skills as a creative artist began to take flight. I started writing professionally for neighborhood newsletters and newspapers. I started performing my original poetry in local coffee shops and bookstores. I started singing original songs any chance I could get. I even managed to interview lots of famous people and slither onto the sets of films and television programs. My work was being seen by thousands of people in my hometown of Philadelphia and surrounding areas.

When I graduated junior high school, which was actually a Montessori school, I knew that my dream was to be in a high school where I could make my writing even better than it was. I was good and I knew it. But I wanted to be even better. I also wanted to be surrounded by people who did what I did. By people with whom I could perhaps collaborate with. By people who were my competition. I certainly didn't want to attend the local high school. The place was named after a man whose anti-violence stance seemed to be ignored by the students and faculty. It was a dangerous place. My friend went there and got assaulted on his first day of school for not giving up his sneaks. It was North Philly. A bad part of town. I wouldn't have lasted a day in that environment. I wouldn't have wanted to even try.

No, the place I longed to be was The City of Brotherly Love Performing Arts Academy. A lot of celebrities went there. That new age doo-wop boy band. That girl from the sitcom about twin brothers switched at birth. A whole lot of talent. And I figured if their spirits could rub off on me just a little bit while I was there, I'd be satisfied. So I applied to the school. But they didn't grant me an interview. All I received was a rejection slip in the mail. No explanation or anything. I knew good and well my portfolio was impressive. I was the youngest accredited member of the press in the city at the time. I was also the youngest filmmaker in the city. I had produced two short films dealing with teen issues. Sex, drugs and booze. That kind of stuff. My work had been featured on every local television news and radio program, and in various publications. A cute kid with a camera. Can't beat that headline.

But what I didn't love was that it was looking like I was going to be forced to attend the 'Let's Make War and Not Love' High School. And I refused hands down to be thrown into such a life-altering position. My mother understood my reluctance to go to a place like that. Our neighborhood was bad enough. We didn't live in the hood. But it wasn't 'Disneyland' either. Apparently they had these rules that you had to attend a certain school depending on where you lived. And my neighborhood school was Hell.

This performing arts school, however, was Heaven. It wasn't a public school. But it wasn't a private school either. A magnet school actually. And they only admitted special students after a long and extensive audition process. A process that took an entire day. But I wasn't even called to come in for an interview. What had I done wrong? Did I misspell something on my application essay? Was my work experience thus far not as astounding as I lead people to believe? Was my punctuation really that awful? I went through as many 'what ifs' as I possibly could, before coming to the conclusion that I wasn't going to let this be the end.

I called the school several times as did my mother. We both requested various times for an interview slot. But each time we were denied. The school claimed there was no additional room for students and that interviews would only be granted for next year's academic cycle. Even though I was informed that a chance existed for me to get into this school next year, I also knew that I could possibly be rejected again. It was time to go to the drawing board. It was time to hatch a plan. Getting into this school was the dream of a lifetime.

Thank goodness for church folk. Thank goodness for family. My family was connected. No, not to the mafia. They were connected to some folks who have some prominence. An elite politician. He held a very high-ranking supervisor position within the city government. I hated to even request such a selfish thing from him. But my guilt over that was short-lived. My main objective was to get into that school. You ever see that film, 'Fame'? Well, much like only the best got into that school, that's how this school was. Anyway, my mother and I managed to get this guy to create the grand maul recommendation letter. He sent it to the school's principal on official city government letterhead. He even carbon copied the document to several of the faculty and staff at the school. Needless to say, my being praised by a dignitary was rather impressive. This didn't get me admitted into the school. But this did get me the interview. But I'm sure that them not accepting me solely upon the recommendation letter was merely a formality. The interview process was tense, tough and long. It was a morning I shall never forget.

My mother and I drove slowly down The Avenue of The Arts. We didn't really have a choice. It was

5

morning rush hour. But I was nervous as I don't know what. The clock near the dashboard said: 8:25. I was supposed to be there at 8:30. I didn't want to be late. If I was late, it would make a really bad impression on the people that'll either say 'yes' or 'no' to my being a part of their student body. We were only like eight blocks away. But traffic was at a standstill. I felt like I was on a Big Apple street corner watching the urban chaos. Cops were in the middle of the street trying to direct traffic, but more so resembling clowns at a toddler's birthday party.

Eventually, I couldn't take the stomach turning suspense of wondering if some miracle was going to get me there on time. So I jumped out the car, blew a kiss to my mom and hightailed it down block after block after block. I was running towards my future.

# CHAPTER 2

# "IN A HOLE, NEED TO DIG OUT"

PHEW! I NEVER THOUGHT the day would actually come. High school graduation. Four years of my life I had spent dealing with cruel adolescents and teenagers making fun of me, and making my life a complete and living hell. But finally it was all over. I was about to begin life as an adult. An adult. That's kind of insane when you think about it. I mean the day before, I was a snot nose fifteen year old. And suddenly I was seventeen. 17! Wow!

Anyway, I applied to a lot of different colleges. Well, actually I'm lying. I wanted to apply to several colleges. But my SAT scores weren't exactly of the utmost caliber. But I don't personally feel that a standardized examination is able to dictate just how much brain power one has. It's a test, simple as that. Some people are horrible at tests. I'm one of those people. Doesn't mean I don't study. Doesn't mean I don't pay attention. Doesn't mean I'm dumb. I'm just bad at them. And what's the point of taking an SAT anyway? I mean, don't we take enough tests in high school as it is?

I was doing okay in school. I wasn't failing anything. Barely got through my algebra classes though. I had taken like two or three developmental math courses, but that hadn't really helped too much. And my algebra teacher (a tall pale man with a stick up his butt), and a weird spiky haired pudgy kid were accusing me of cheating on an exam. If it weren't for Mrs. Myles, I don't think I'd have been able to survive a minute of my time spent with decimals, timetables and exponents. And as far as those accusations of classroom dishonesty? Total lack of validity.

My principal told me that perhaps I was spending too much time focusing my attention on my major. At the academy, my major was writing/television production. My guidance counselor basically in so many words had assured me, that where I wanted to go would probably not be a feasible option. That's really friggin' encouraging coming from someone who was supposed to be helping me. But I'd be remiss not to admit that I didn't really possess much school spirit. It took personal political connections to get me in that school in the first place. I JUST HAD TO GO THERE! But before I got there, I had to spend a year somewhere else.

Looking for a school for my freshman year was a pain in the butt. I was in a hole, and didn't know how to dig myself out. School was starting in a month. And still, I didn't have one yet. At least not one that I was satisfied with. My mother began an exhaustive search for a private school to send me to. She even considered for a moment shipping me to a boarding school in West Chester. Not because I was bad or anything. I was far from that. But ultimately, she changed her mind. I'm not sure why. But I think it was because she felt she'd miss me. After all, it was just she and I.

My mom first located a Catholic preparatory school in Chestnut Hill. This school had a strict uniform policy. Sorry, no can do. The uniforms were a caustic red and blue. I needed to have my freedom. Plus, they wanted me to get rid of the rag tail in the back of my head. That little tail was my trademark during my youth. I had it ever since I was two. And I'd cry if the barber would mistakenly trim it. There was no way I was destroying it with evil blades. The second school she found was a small high school in Northeast Philly, which had about a hundred students in total. It wasn't the performing arts academy, and it certainly wasn't my cup of tea. But the administrators there were cool people, that I must say. They were all of the Caucasian persuasion, and were tremendously incredibly the nicest bunch of people one could ever meet. The secretaries were so cool that some days I'd miss the first bus at the corner by the 7-11 because I'd be engaged in conversation.

Of course one might say that I've always had a social interaction difficulty. But I'm able to relate better to people who are twenty or thirty years my senior. I don't know, I just feel more comfortable socializing with more mature individuals. Most kids my age would rather gossip about who the lovely ladies of The Pussycat Dolls are dating. But me, I'd rather discuss the state of the world, which for as long as I can remember has always been in peril. And it doesn't seem like that's going to change anytime soon. Don't get me wrong, it's not like I'm always serious. It's not like I never get crazy or goofy. I'm as goofy as they come. But I'm a super serious person, too. Probably has something to do with my Zodiac sign. I'm Aquarius. Born on an extremely important day in February. None other than the day of the Groundhog. People always find that amusing. Every time I have a birthday, first thing people ask me is if I saw my shadow. I think it's cool.

So after awhile, I began to experience the pitfalls of attending a school for what is basically to help prepare young individuals who need a special kind of help. Not mentally ill kids or anything. But kids who come from households full of despair, poverty, and abuse and whatnot. Every other day there were bomb threats. Students sprayed mace and other types of pepper spray into the ventilation system causing the entire school building (which again was very miniscule), to become filled with an eye-stinging, smoky mess. Kids threw soda cans and other items at the backs of the instructors' heads, when their backs were turned as they wrote on the blackboards. And sometimes these kids were bold enough to even throw items at the instructors' heads, when they were facing the class. They were loud, rambunctious and just plain rude.

These kids could have cared less that some of us actually wanted to learn. Thankfully, I was amongst a feeble few who did want to be educated. But my peers hardly ever exercised their personal voice to exterminate the major distractions that stood in the way of receiving a quality education. And I, as a freshman, despite my strong willed content of character, was reluctant to be as vocal as I could be. I guess I was leery about being too vocal until I had observed my atmosphere for awhile, and become accustomed to how things were in this domain.

It was fortunate, however, that I soon learned a relative of mine was a fellow peer. This made me feel not as alone as I previously did. But Elise wasn't that close to me. Plus, she had problems of her own. She was 16 and pregnant. And if you knew her, you'd know why. The girl was incredibly beautiful. Five feet something, straight and long brown hair, brown eyes and a smile that could melt the sun. But the baby's daddy was not in the picture. She was alone. Except for her parents who thankfully didn't give up on her. Yet, it really didn't seem that we were on the same page. I didn't go out of my way to connect with her, nor did she with me. I think if it were meant for me to associate with her other than the typical cordial salutations, it would have been so.

I went to the interview for high school with my portfolio. And I had to take some writing tests and come up with stories off the cuff in a limited amount of time. I belonged at that school. It was my destiny. Without me, that school would have been a puzzle with a missing piece. I guess that letter helped somewhat. Because before I knew it, I was officially a student.

Now my high school years had come to a close. I threw my cap into the air and hung my gown up to dry. I was an educated boy. Now it was time for me to become an educated man. I had some intentions of applying to Morehouse or Howard. Even a career in law was something I'd had on my mind since I was seven years old. But when I turned 12 and figured out that maybe I was put on this planet to entertain and educate, that became my life's focus. My aspirations were, and still are very clear. I know what I want to do. And I'll be doing everything humanly possible to make all of my aspirations come to fruition.

Philly was my hometown. Still is. I wasn't sure if I wanted to leave it. In fact, I knew I didn't want to leave it. Yet, I also knew that sometimes you have to go somewhere else in order to come back home. But I really didn't go out of my way to submit applications to a lot of schools. My guidance counselor told me not to bother. Plus, I guess I sort of naively figured that somehow I'd automatically fall into the hands of an angel. I was a filmmaker. I wanted to be amongst the NYU elite. Or the folks at UCLA or USC. But all these schools were beyond the finances I could muster.

I am the product of a single parent home. And though my grandparents helped out in any way they possibly could, we're talking about college education here. That doesn't come cheap for people who don't have a trust fund or wealthy legal guardians. And scholarships? Well, I could forget that. I wasn't the worst student. But I wasn't Valedictorian either. So where could I go? I was a black boy. There was no question that my future was undertaking courses in a higher education atmosphere. Black men in America who don't have a Diploma, and/or a Degree, is a recipe for disaster. I realized that. My mother constantly reinforced that in me. But it was something that regardless, would stay embedded in my brain forever.

I had previously visited a few schools. I'll never forget how beautiful the campus of Howard looked. And the cafeteria was amazing compared to the little café at high school. And the people. There were a lot of students. But they all seemed like family, and I was just a guest in their house. But still something in my gut told me not to invest my future in a predominately black school.

I grew up in the North Philly section of the city. Urban. Not the hood. But some days it was close to it. But through extra curricular activities, internships and arts jobs, I managed to surround myself with an eclectic group comprised of various sizes, shapes, colors and persuasions. So I wasn't sure if I wanted to spend the next four years of my life surrounded by people who look like me. This world is a rainbow. Not just one color.

Time flew and flew. And I hadn't made a decision. Two schools had rejected me. I wasn't knowledgeable about the film programs of Drexel and Temple Universities. I heard things, but never really fully investigated. So my mother, who has always been my personal life manager, would make the decision for me. I trusted her judgment. My grandparents had moved down to South Carolina. And there was a small little black school down there that had a film program. And my cousin worked there as a security guard. I didn't exactly jump at the idea of packing up and heading south. But I didn't balk at the idea either. Not because I was half and half on the idea. Believe me, I wasn't. Moving down south and attending a black school was not my desire. But there was no place else to go. And I hadn't really made a major effort to find an alternative.

My dream schools were in the multi-thousands. And my pockets were in the multi-empties. So off I went. It was the end, and the beginning.

# CHAPTER 3

# "YOU'RE GOING TO BE LATE"

MY MOTHER, MY GRANDPARENTS, and I approached the campus in my grandfather's red Cadillac. My stomach was in knots. My lips were poked. My mouth was silent. My eyes were drooped in mourn. A gospel song was playing on the radio. I was in the back seat with my mother who was extremely miffed at me. During the whole twenty-minute ride from my grandparents' house in Manning, South Carolina to campus a few miles away, my mother was periodically yelling at me for having a negative attitude about things. My grandmother kept asking if I really wanted to go to college. Annoyed, I kept telling her that of course I wanted to go. But I guess my attitude was saying something else.

At breakfast that morning, I was even more in my own world. It took everything out of my family to even get me out of bed. I purposely didn't set the alarm, and I prayed that the alarms would go off late for everyone else. I figured maybe I could delay my first day of school by one day. But it didn't work. My grandmother knocked on my bedroom door and yelled for me to wake up. But I laid there facing the opposite side of the room, pretending to be deaf. She called for me once more and then gave up. My mom was next. She intentionally made a whole bunch of noise, knocking on the wall. She even shoved me a few times. I groggily told her that I'd be getting up soon. She believed me and departed. But twenty-minutes expired, and I was still submerged under a mountain of covers. Next was my grandfather. And he didn't play. He yelled so loud with such a distinct pounding voice, I didn't have a choice but to at least sit up in bed. I told him that I'd be getting up soon.

"You're going to be late!" he yelled.

"I know. I know. I'll be up in a minute." I responded.

"Babs is making pancakes. Aren't you going to eat?"

Babs is my grandmom. Short for Barbara. But I call her Mom-Mom.

"Yes, I'm going to eat." I said, slowly getting out of bed at the pace of a snail.

But that wasn't enough for Pop-Pop. Oh yeah, that's what I call my grandfather. His real name is James. He stood there, just staring at me. His large bifocals covering his eyes. His head nodded with disgust. And a perturbed sigh escaped his lips. He eventually gave up and walked out in a huff. He always gave me that long hard glance when he wanted me to know that I wasn't acting in a manner that he deemed respectable. It always worked, too. But I would never admit to him that he was right and I was wrong. What kid wants to admit when he's wrong?

After several more minutes of reluctance to begin my higher education at a black school, I finally got up all the way and headed to the bathroom to groom myself. But even this I did extremely slowly. Every moment painful. What had I been thinking back in high school? Why had I not made a more conscious effort to get into a school of my choosing? Why had I not been equipped with an IQ that would have enabled me to get a perfect score on the SATs, which in turn would have subsequently given me the opportunity to shine at a school that would make my dreams come true?

After I showered and dressed, I sat down to the kitchen table to feast upon two golden delicious homemade pancakes. But even the scrumptious cuisine was not enough to make me feel better about my impending trip to doom. But rather than voice my feelings, which would not have really made any difference since reality was set in stone, I instead was silent minus a few occasional huffs and puffs.

We pulled up to the security booth of the campus. The guard (my cousin Paul), welcomed us with a friendly smile. All my parental units smiled back. I frowned, but was cordial. And we cruised on through amongst a sea of cars, trucks, moving vans, and other vehicles. We parked in the lot by the school gymnasium. My folks got out of the car, but I stayed inside. Nodding my head to myself. Contemplating. Worrying about the next four months of my life. Could I really survive this, I wondered. Could I survive being away from my zone of comfort? Could I survive being somewhere I'd rather not be? I was literally frightened to get out of the car. My family stood outside the vehicle with drawn eyes and tapping feet.

# CHAPTER 4

# "BLACK PEOPLE!"

BLACK PEOPLE! BLACK PEOPLE! Black people everywhere. Obviously this means I got out of the car. A large gym was almost indescribable. Extremely spacious, except I could hardly tell how spacious, since the basketball court was filled with hundreds of young people and their families waiting to register for school and classes. There was what seemed like tons of bleachers that were several feet high. A small campus. But a big gym.

My folks and I signed a roster and then sat down amongst the other awaiting would-be scholars. I was still silent. But the noise of the crowd ruined any chance of me being able to meditate. I could feel dozens of eyes on me. Haven't you ever noticed how black people look at you? They just stare. We stared back. I guess we were sizing each other up, you know? Trying to figure out what each other were like. If we were cool. Or if we were snobs. If we were urban. Or if we were sophisticated. If we were smart. Or if we were ignorant.

I was a freshman. I guess I was sort of intimidated by my surroundings and the people in it. Not sort of. Colossally intimidated. Not just by the people who were soon to become my peers. But by the administrators and those in leadership positions, too. They were all seated at various tables. All types. Some hard looking. Some potentially inviting ones. But they were all hard to make. It was first sight. I wasn't a psychic. I couldn't read minds. But I was always an observer. So I guess it was in my nature to worry what they might be like. How they might treat me. And worried about my impending first contact with each of them. In my book first impressions last a lifetime. I mean, I could have cared less what they thought of me. I was worried about my perceptions of them.

Mom-Mom was chatting with another woman around her age. She always managed to find a friend amongst strangers. She's a southern belle. That means she's a talker. I don't know what she was talking about. I couldn't hear her. But I really didn't want to hear her. Because I could imagine what she was telling this lady. She was probably boasting about how her grandson was going to be going to school down there. She was proud. I got that. And I hated upsetting her. But if she expected me to act like I really wanted to be there, that wasn't going to happen. Because then I would have been lying.

What's the point of my being dishonest about my feelings? If I would have done that, I would have simply been deceiving people but feeling really bad inside. Would that be fair? Should my own happiness and stability be compromised in order to make someone else feel content? Even if that person is a relative, I think not. I love my grandmother. I really do. But either I was going to tell the truth, or just do what I was raised to do. 'If you don't have anything nice to say, then don't say anything at all'. That's what my mother has always told me. So you know what? That's what I did. Kept my lips sealed. At least for the time being.

The rest of the time spent in the gym lasted for hours and hours. When my family and I finally got to the table to register for my classes, we sat down with the woman who would be my underclassman advisor, Ms. Johnson. She seemed nice enough. Of course she wasn't really engaged in a conversation with me. She was more interested in discussing the weather with, you guessed it, Mom-Mom. And they were really talking about it, too. It wasn't one of those ice-breaker conversations that we human beings sometimes initiate as we prepare to pass the time while handling business. No, this was serious. You'd think the two of them were in Al Roker's entourage. It was insane.

While chatting with Mom-Mom, Ms. Johnson inputted my name onto the rosters for:

1. Freshman Orientation, 2. Freshman Composition, 3. College Algebra, 4. American History I, 5. Music Appreciation.

She informed me that it would probably be in my best interest to take fourteen credits that semester. I explained that my mathematical skills were like that of a person without mental stability being in the Oval Office. She assured me that there were tutoring programs on campus and teachers who were more than willing to help me when needed.

"When needed?" I replied, "That would be 24:7. I am dumb in math. I just don't get it. Math doesn't like me. I used to not like math. But I've conquered being afraid of it. I just know that I suck at it. Trust me, it's going to take a lot more than tutoring to get me to pass college algebra."

I went to a Montessori school for much of my life. From pre-school on. Don't get me wrong. I loved every minute of it. But the way they taught me math was done so in a fashion that at hindsight was non-beneficial for me. As a kid it was fun pushing the little blue and red beads on the stick with my miniature fingertips, and counting them. But as time progressed, I was never really taught math. And up to this point with the exception of Mrs. Myles, who taught me developmental math, no one has really successfully managed to make me understand how mathematics operates. And thinking about it, maybe my brain just isn't conditioned to understand it.

I'm sorry, but I feel like as long as I'm able to count all the dead presidents in my wallet, which as of now tally zero, then that's all that matters. I have no desire to be a doctor or scientist. What do I need all this math for? I'm not an imbecile. I realize that we use math every day. There's not really anything that we humanly do where math is not in some way a part of it. However, for the average individual to actually recognize the math in our daily lives is just not reality.

Mom-Mom and my mother turned up their noses at me. They were angry at my negative energy. But I didn't look at it as negative energy. I looked at it as truth. They tried to blow off my comments by changing the subject, and inquiring about how the other classes would be constructed. I could tell that they were embarrassed by my behavior. I didn't think I was wrong in what I said. If I was coming off as a pessimistic youth, that wasn't my intention.

Pop-Pop just sat there, silent. Trying to mentally transport himself into another dimension.. He had a small little booklet in his hand. I think it was Pander College's 'Rules on Campus Behavior' and junk like that. Stuff I didn't really need to pay attention to. Because even though I'm opinionated and temperamental, I've always been a good kid at heart. A goody two shoes as they say.

Ms. Johnson printed out my schedule and handed it to my mom. My mom handed it to me. I took it and began folding it. About to stuff it in my pocket. But my mom yanked it out of my hand and scolded me for not treating it with care.

"Adam," she said, and not in the tone of someone who's joyful, "Put it in the folder the man gave you when you got in line. Don't get it all wrinkled."

So of course I listened to my mom. Those piercing eyes of hers would make any person succumb to her demands. I wasn't balling up the schedule as a sign of protest or anything. And it's not that I didn't care. I just wasn't thinking. I knew this was the last place on earth I wanted to be. And I guess I was just preparing to stuff it in my pocket as an inadvertent symbol of my emotion for being a part of something I didn't want to be a part of.

Anyway, my family and I stood up and thanked Ms. Johnson. Then we moved to the next table. And the next. And the next. Signing paperwork, reading over materials. Yada yada yada. Eventually we came to the school photographer. He asked me to stand in front of a large blue screen. I reluctantly complied. He held up his camera and told me to smile. My folks were watching. But nothing in the world could make me smile at that moment. I frowned. Maybe the photographer thought it was a smile because he snapped the picture anyway. And that was that. Flash. Bam! Done. He printed out the photograph and laminated my identification badge.

The photographer handed me the badge. I didn't even look at it. Mom-Mom asked to see it. She didn't even give me a chance to present it to her. She just snatched it. Not violently. Just with her infamous swift maternal intensity. She looked at it and her face crunched.

"Let me see it," My mom said. She looked at it and she too, frowned.

Pop-Pop was next to peruse it.

"Why didn't you smile?" he asked.

"I don't know." I said, under my breath.

"You look mad at the world." My mom said.

I'm not mad at the world. At the moment, I'm mad at you. Of course I didn't tell my mother this. But I was. I really was. I resented that she and my grandparents were making me go to this school. I didn't want to be there. And as far as I was concerned, this was temporary. I didn't know how, but I was getting out of there as soon as I possibly could.

# CHAPTER 5

# "A BOTTLE, AND I WAS THE GENIE"

POP-POP DOUBLE-PARKED THE CAR in front of a two-story residence hall called Chesterfield. Named after one of the school's former Presidents. I happened to come across that bit of information as I haphazardly read one of the school's manuals.

My folks and I began grabbing some of my belongings. TV, VCR, sheets, garment and luggage bags, etc. We entered the building where a middle-aged black woman greeted us. She had curly bronze tinted hair. Her name was Mrs. Davis. Immediately the woman struck a conversation with my grandmother. No surprise there. She handed me a clipboard with some housing forms for me to sign. After I gave my John Hancock, she gave me a key. Pop-Pop and my mother followed me down a long corridor. I occasionally bumped shoulders with other soon to be dorm mates.

Room 106. Tiny. A jail cell. A bottle. And I was the genie. Tan cement walls. Two desks, two chairs. At least there was a large window, which faced the front of the building. Through it I could see grass, trees, students, and cars. I turned to face the left side of the room, where the bed was located next to the wooden closet and sink, below a wall mirror. But on the bed were mountains of gigantic jeans, sweats, and jerseys. Man! I wanted that side of the room. I mean, since I had to live there for awhile. So my family and I were forced to put my stuff on the bed to the right side of the room. An empty mattress stained with urine and some other DNA.

"We're going to have to get some cleaning stuff." I told my mom, "This place is a pig sty."

I'm not a neat freak or anything. But I can't stand mess either. It's the Aquarius in me. It's the Mom-Mom in me. It's the Rochelle in me. Rochelle, that's my aunt, my mom's sister. Rochelle is the oldest. I love her to death. But she's quite the obsessive compulsive. I guess I get my obsessive compulsive tendencies from her. She wakes up in the morning and the very first thing she does is come down the stairs, and raise the blinds to about three or four feet exact from the windowsill. Then she straightens the pillows on the sofa. And God forbid, if anyone has moved a picture frame by just an inch or two, my auntie will know.

Mom-Mom finally entered the room all in smiles, boasting about how big the room was. Was she kidding? Oh my God. This room wasn't big enough for the mouse that probably lived there. There were some droppings in the corner by the closet. I guess Mom-Mom was just trying to be optimistic. Or either she was in denial. I just shook my head and rolled my eyes. How was I supposed to live there? Aaagh! So my folks and I headed back out to retrieve some things to make the dorm room more habitable. Upon return, I was left to fend for myself. My folks were on their way back home. But for me, this *was* home. Unfortunately.

I swept. I scrubbed. I washed. I sponged. I wiped. I shoveled dust balls and dirt into a dustpan and emptied them into my small trashcan by the door. I sprayed the window with Windex. I sprayed polish on the furniture. I placed sheets over the mattress. I placed a few air freshening devices in the room. One above my bed. And one near my mystery roommate's bed.

Mystery roommate. Hmm. Now that I was done, I figured I could investigate who my roommate was. I snooped around a bit. Not anything devious. I didn't creep in other people's property or anything. Just surfed the room with my eyes. And on his desk behind some books and folders, I discovered a picture frame. Inside the frame was a photograph. A photograph of a family of four. A mom. Dad. Teenage male. Tween-age girl. All African-American. Seemed like a decent looking family. I was hoping they had me roomed with someone with whom I could at least co-exist. We didn't have to be best friends. But we should at least be able to live with each other, without major issue.

I connected my phone to the wall and immediately called my folks. They asked how I was doing. I told them I was fine. But I was lying. I'm sure they could tell by the anxiety ridden inflection in my voice. But they weren't going to baby me either. So we chatted for a few moments and then I hung up. I turned on the television in hopes of finding a program or movie that would help me escape from reality for awhile. I flipped and flipped. It was early evening so there wasn't really much on. A couple of news shows. Some talk shows. Jerry Springer. But that didn't really interest me. At least not at the moment. So I turned off the television and instead just let the blank screen watch me. Silence is golden. But I didn't feel rich.

# CHAPTER 6

# "HI, MY NAME IS…"

THE DOOR TO MY room slowly opened. In walked a kid around eighteen. He was tall and dark. Had wavy hair and a thin moustache. He was wearing a blue jersey, blue bandanna, and blue jeans. A couple of his teeth were gold. With him were a couple of his boys in similar urban gear. He nodded to me. I nodded back. But he didn't really introduce himself. I figured maybe he'd do that later when his boys weren't with him. They all sat down and started blasting his CD player apparently not noticing that I now had my television on again. I was still letting it watch me, but I could slightly hear Roseanne yelling at Becky and Darlene.

I kind of cut my eyes at the guys in slight anger. No, not anger. Just annoyance. The nerve of them. But my roommate nor his cronies seemed to notice. Or if they did, they just didn't care. So I sat up in my bed, and acted like I was really paying attention to the laugh out loud comedy on the tube. Even though I wasn't really trying to be entertained. I'd have rather just sat and wallowed in self-pity.

Eventually the visitors departed. And now it was just he and I. Me and my roomy. He walked over and stuck out his hand.

"Yo, wassup?" he said.

"Hey, how's it going?" I responded, shaking his hand in what I thought was a cool way of greeting someone. But my handshake with a few extra moves of the fingers was so old school, it made his eyes bug out in disbelief. But he made those protruding eyes of his disappear quickly, so as not to make me feel too embarrassed.

"I'm Dustin." he said to me.

"Adam."

"Cool. You a freshman?"

"Yeah. You?"

"Second semester."

"Oh."

Not at all a particularly interesting conversation, right? It was one of those conversations that were just completely awkward. We were strangers forced to live with each other. Like 'The Real World'. I could instantly tell that we were from totally different sides of the road. He was urban. That's my word for ghetto. It's just something about the word 'ghetto' I can't stand. I feel like I'm being racist or something using the word 'ghetto'. Being prejudiced against my own race, you know? And I'm not like that. But I guess the word 'urban' could be considered different things by different people. I mean: maybe compared to a white person, I'm urban. Anyway, he was urban. And I was…well, I wasn't.

I wasn't exactly sub-urban. But I'm sort of sophisticated. Reserved, respectful, and dignified. Now I couldn't really tell if Dustin lacked those qualities. It would take some time for me to observe his behavior before I could decode what kind of person he was. But for some reason he didn't seem like the type of person I'd be able to talk politics with, you know? He seemed like the type of person that would find discussing the President and our country's wars with other countries extremely monotonous. I know they say: 'Don't judge a book by its cover.' But sometimes the cover of a book is so creatively designed that you know the book is an appealing read. And other times it's so poorly done, you know it's bound to be a debacle.

Now, Pander College was a respectable community. It was a religious campus that placed strong emphasis on the church, the gospel, and living and doing right by God. This meant that the reputation of the school as a whole couldn't be compromised by a student's actions. If some type of incident ever took place it was crucial to isolate, confine, and conjure solutions in a timely fashion. This meant that with such a strong responsibility for students to embrace, that of carrying out the mission of this educational body, it was important that we represent our school in the best of light.

No pants hanging below our butts. No hats on inside the building. And Mrs. Davis placed signs around the dorm encouraging us to wear business attire as often as we could. Profanity was prohibited. No du-rags. No alcohol. No smoking in residence halls and campus offices. And from what I had been reading, Freshman Orientation was meant to help me prepare for dealing with these issues that semester.

Of course I really didn't need all that instruction. Much of it was common sense. But if you've never been away from home and maybe if you've lived in a sheltered environment all your life, perhaps you've never gotten the basic home training of dealing with the reactions of others as well as the consequences of each of your actions. Little did I know, Dustin would test those murky waters time and time again.

# CHAPTER 7

# "CAUGHT RED HANDED"

MY FIRST DAY OF school. Over and done with. Hadn't even taken a class yet and already I felt utterly exhausted. I was in bed wearing my pajamas. I turned to look at my alarm clock. It said: 8:30pm. Time for some shut-eye. I curled under my covers, slightly shivering. The air conditioner was on full blast. Whoo! I rested my head against my two fluffed up pillows and closed my weary eyes. Off to the land of la-la.

BANG! BANG! I groggily awakened to a pounding sound. I turned to look at my alarm clock. It said: 12:15am. I yawned and then turned on my desk lamp. I squinted my eyes, trying to become adjusted to the lighting shift in the room. And then I noticed a dimly lit face pressed against my window. The face belonged to Dustin. He was holding a bottle of beer and his eyes were intoxicated red. I already knew what he wanted.

He couldn't articulate his desire. But I knew what he was begging for. It was fifteen minutes after the strict curfew mandated by the school administration, for freshman and first year transfer students to be back in their residence halls. He wanted me to let him in because the front door was locked. And if he knocked on that door then he knew our dorm mother would chew him out. Mrs. Davis seemed pretty okay. But I could tell she wasn't the type to play around, or let things just simply slide.

But I was new to this roommate scenario. I'm an only child. I wasn't used to having to do things like this. If I were to let him in, I could be reprimanded by the administration for being an accomplice. But if I were to keep him outside, what might he do to me? If he got a bad first impression of me, that wouldn't be a good thing. It would mean that we'd be down each other's throats on a constant basis. I didn't want that. There was already enough drama in the simple fact that I had to go to this school. Adding fuel to the fire would only make me an arsonist.

So I hopped out of bed and over to the window, still semi-conscious. I wiped the sandman from the sides of my eyes. I strained to hear Dustin's voice through the glass. But like I said, I knew what he wanted. So I grabbed my room key and slowly opened the door to the hallway. I looked around and went to the main lobby. I looked over at the front desk and saw that Mrs. Davis' office door was locked. I looked around once more. Just making sure I wasn't about to be caught red-handed.

Dustin's face was now pressed against the door. His right hand was barely clutching the door handle. I opened the door and the smell of whisky, or rum, or something (I don't drink so I don't know the difference), leaped right out of his mouth and into my nostrils. My eyes started to pop into the back of my head, taken aback by the less than appealing aroma. He grabbed my shoulder and sort of escorted me down the hall. Well really, I was escorting him. But even in his half drunken state, he seemed to be leading somehow. With both of us practically knocked out for two completely different reasons, we were quite a pair. We got back to the room. He fell into bed. I fell into mine.

# CHAPTER 8

"SAME BLOOD"

"MURDER YOUR FEAR." SHE said, while writing that sentence and subsequent ones on the blackboard, "Murder your fear of mathematics. It is crucial that you realize just how important mathematics is, as it relates to our daily lives. Everything we do. Everything. It is all determined by mathematics and science. By numbers and characters."

Those were the words of my algebra teacher. My first day of classes. My first class of the day. What a class to wake up to at 8 o'clock in the morning. I woke up out of a great sleep. I ruined the ecstasy of being in bed snuggled up with a warm companion, my pillow. I ruined utopia and tranquility. For math. Okay, enough of my complaints. It was time. It was time for me to face reality. Reality being, I had to take this class and I had to do well, or else I was going to fail. But this wasn't high school. If I failed anything in college, that would be the end of me. People generally don't give a damn about how your scores are in high school once you have college transcripts. You're a kid in high school. You're a man (or woman), in college.

But here's the problem. Math has always been my greatest challenge in life. No, really it has. I used to be deathly afraid of it. Scared to the point where I would just give up simply at the sight of an equation. But a tutor (a family friend), managed to actually help me overcome my fear. Actually, it was probably her curvaceous beauty that helped contribute to my tentative mathematical success. That, and the sincere assistance from Mrs. Myles, and the folks at Sylvan Learning Center.

But just because you're not afraid of something anymore doesn't mean you're out of the woods. You may have conquered a phobia. Say your phobia is the fear of rodents. And perhaps, one day you pick up a mouse and you're not shivering or fidgeting like you used to. Great, right? But does that mean you want to go around picking up mice for the rest of your life? Not this guy. No how, no way. I guess what I'm trying to say is, even though I'm not afraid of it anymore, math is still my enemy.

I hoped that this algebra teacher would make good of the name: 'teacher'. Because that's what I needed. Someone who could actually teach me. I was just leery about being overly optimistic about that hope coming true. I wasn't the only student in class. It was a small room in the Vance Science building. And it seemed like they jammed all two-thousand plus students in this one room. How in the world was Ms. Hinson going to be able to focus on little ol' me when she had all these other students?

Wait a minute! Hinson? Hmm. I wondered if we could be related. This could be the best thing that could happen to me. Was the person about to teach me, be someone who has the same blood as I? No, this couldn't be happening. This would be too weird of a coincidence. I thought my cousin Paul was the only kin of mine that worked at the school. If this woman was my family, this class might be a breeze. I mean I didn't expect to be allowed to just sit around and do nothing, and still expect to pass the class. But if this was true, at least I could imagine I'd have a little more space when it comes to her badgering her students to learn and learn quick.

So I was right. And I was wrong. Our blood may have been connected. But that didn't make me special. Matter of fact it seemed like she was hardest on me. I was trying. Really, I was. But I just couldn't get it. And it just seemed like she was going a mile a minute. I couldn't keep up. My mind was a blank. The girl to my left seemed to get it just fine. I kind of looked on with her as she scribbled notes in her composition book. I was trying to see if I could figure out how she was doing the calculations. She kind of gave me the eye. You know, kind of like the eye my mom gives me when she's not a happy camper.

"Can't you do your own work?" she asked me.

"I'm trying. I just can't figure it out." I answered.

"Well, I might be able to help you out after class. But I don't want to get in trouble for talking to you right now."

"Okay. Cool beans. Name's Adam. You?"

"Wildflower Cheyenne."

Wildflower. Interesting. She was a beautiful Native American girl. Not bad on the eyes at all. So I know what you're thinking. A banging female offered to help me after class. I bet you're wondering if we studied math, or if we studied *something else*. I'm not even going to lie. The girl was sexy as hell. But I'm not really the flirting type whatsoever. And more importantly, I just don't have time for that. Not for the women. The best way for me to get out of that place was to do well. And the only way I could do that, was to keep my mind focused on the main reason why I was ultimately there. And that was to get an education in order to get out. Of course that didn't mean I couldn't look. And believe me, I looked. And I looked hard.

But I looked at her in secret. I'm a private person. If you ever catch my eye wandering, then you have accomplished a major feat. See, most guys my age…hell, most guys period, will break their necks to check out a female. And they'll whistle and make catcalls. And they'll just be staring at their backsides like a cheese steak from Tony Luke's. And I always hear my boys make comments like: 'Yo, girl, you got a fat ass!', 'Damn, I gotta hit that.', and 'She got mad chest.' And lots of other things that I don't even want to mention because they're just too vulgar. I mean, look, there's nothing wrong with checking out the honeys. And if that's the way you want to do it, then fine. But me, I'm not like that. I'm a gentleman. Some ladies like that loud type of attention. But that's not the type of lady I'm interested in. And during that time, I wasn't interested in any. I just didn't have the time. I was married to school.

So Wildflower tutored me for awhile. And even though she tried sincerely, I just couldn't get it. I worked some with Ms. Hinson, too. But she still moved too fast for me. Or maybe it was just that she couldn't really break it down for me in laymen's terms. That's what I really needed. I took test after test. And pretty much failed test after test. She allowed me to make them up. But that didn't really help. Thankfully, we had a few group projects that helped me raise my grade somewhat. And I took advantage of as many extra credit opportunities as I possibly could. So that helped the grade, too. Midterms came and went. And then came finals. I cringed during the entire 1 hour and thirty minute examination. One hundred questions. 100! But I managed to get through it. Barely. I got a 'D'. Passing for this college. But for me, it was as good as an 'F'.

# CHAPTER 9

# "BLUE"

SOMETHING WOKE ME UP. Not my alarm clock. It was too early. It must have been my biological clock buzzing. I slowly opened my eyes. Something…a little voice or something told me to look up. I strained to look up at my forehead where I noticed two red dots slightly dancing upon my skin. I turned to my left to find Dustin sitting in Indian style on his bed, aiming one black firearm at me and polishing another with a white cloth. On his face was a smile a mile wide. Not one of a satanic nature. But playful, childlike. And either I was in a state of freshman mentality (meaning I just didn't care that a gun was pointed at me), I was traumatized, or I was just too tired to even comprehend the serious nature of the situation. We exchanged no dialogue. He stopped using me as a playtime target practice and I turned back in bed towards the gray concrete wall. But my eyes weren't closed. At least not both of them. From then on, I slept with one eye ajar.

The following morning I awoke to emptiness. The scolding sun was breaking in through the blinds on the window. My gun-touting roommate was missing in action. Maybe he's in the shower, I thought. His bed was neatly made. Maybe he went to class. I immediately popped out of bed and ran over to my closet. I took out my video camera and began rolling tape. Of the two boxes of ammunition in his dresser drawer. And under his socks: two large plastic bags filled with a white powdery substance and pieces of black electrical tape on the bottom left hand corners.

I wanted to get footage of his weapons, too. But alas, I couldn't. He wasn't stupid enough to leave them out in the open. And if they were around, they were hiding extremely well. But I knew that he had to have those guns for a purpose. And I assumed that it wasn't for hunting squirrel. And if that's the case, I figured he probably carried them on his person in case he had to shoot someone. You're probably wondering why I videotaped all his stuff, right? Well, did you really expect me to stay in a room with someone, and not at least assemble some evidence that proves I'm not privy to their felonies? I just lived there. I refused to be guilty by association.

It wasn't long before I discovered what was right in front of my face from day one. My roommate wasn't the average roommate. He wasn't some average guy. He was from Cali. But not the glamorous and glitzy part if you catch my drift. Palm trees didn't exist in his neck of the woods. And if they did, trust me, they were severely overshadowed by the darkness that surrounded the type of lifestyle he lead. You would never have guessed it from his demeanor. I sure wasn't suspicious. Despite his urbanism, he seemed like a regular guy.

Dustin's mom called him every day. And he even still called her 'mommy'. He sounded like a cute little kid saying it. Sort of immature like, you know? And his girlfriend called him all the time. *And his girlfriend called him all the time.* No, I didn't repeat myself. He had two of them. He probably had a whole bunch. I think he was a major playa. Anyway, we weren't friends or anything. Just roommates. But occasionally he'd tell me about his record company. He claimed he had an independent hip-hop recording studio back home, and he was considering merging business with his homeys in New York. I asked to hear some of his stuff, but he never let me. He let me read some things though. Some poetry. Dude was a major poet. A real romantic. You should have seen how the girls were eating right from his hands. How they went crazy over his pen. His words were beautiful though.

### *Love Pulls Us*
### *By Dustin Cooke*

Like the stinger of an angry yellowjacket
Your love pierces me
Because I know your love is also hate
Built on the intensity of your emotions and feelings

For me
Both you and I together, thrive on dysfunction
But if we try to part ways
It's like we're pulled closer
Like suction
Love pulls us
Like Sabrina, the little neighborhood girl
Pulling her little curly haired brother
In a little red wagon down the block

His writing skills might one day garner him a Pulitzer. I knew it even then. But that didn't erase the real him. Dustin wore blue. A blue bandanna. And the guy across the hall and the one next door wore red. Red bandannas. In other words, I didn't know what color I should wear in order to be safe around there. Granted, we weren't on so-called gangland turf. However, terrorists made war on American soil, not just on their own. So I suppose Dustin and all his co gang-bangers could do the same.

Now, don't get me wrong. He didn't scare me one bit. He was a nice guy really. But I just have a little issue living with someone who kills people for the sport of it. For the chance to get a tat on their shoulder. Or a bullet hole in the side of their neck. And all this to signify receipt of trophies for their kill. All this simply to prove manhood and allegiance. But allegiance to what, to whom? Other people like him who murders cops and people just to do it? Kill because you walk down the street wearing the wrong color? I mean it's not just red and blue. The Bloods and Crips aren't the only gangs that exist in the world. So the only way we all can really have some element of safety in our daily lives, is if we just walk around in our birthday suits.

I suppose that my frequent lack of sleep was a bad case of insomnia. Even though it started at the beginning of college, I'm sure it was only strengthened by my subconscious fear of living with someone who murders kids and manages to sleep at night. But it wasn't something that was always on my mind. I just didn't sleep. Simple as that. So instead, I just watched television into the wee hours of the morning. Or wrote. Probably the only thing Dustin and I had in common was the fact that we were both writers. If it weren't for his um…profession, I might have considered collaborating with him on something. But, another place. Another time. Little did I know, I was the last person that needed to be worried about some type of an attack on me. I mean it's not like I told anyone about Dustin and his contraband. Not even Mrs. Davis. I just collected the evidence in case. And I'd have rather not become involved with any type of drama involving people with guns and people without a conscience. But it's what happened next that shocked me.

Mrs. Davis informed me one day that while the custodian was doing his early morning rounds on a cool November morning in the lobby, a bucket of urine was dumped on him.

"I don't understand." I told her, "Someone threw a bucket of pee on him?"

"Seems so", Mrs. Davis responded. "No one wants to admit to seeing it happen. But I know Mattie (the custodian) wouldn't lie about something like that."

A more thorough investigation by campus security revealed that Dustin was in fact guilty of what he was accused of. I assume it was some sort of gang initiation or fraternity thing, I don't know. He got suspended from classes for a week. But he didn't stay in the dorm. I don't know if they wouldn't allow him to, or if he just chose to stay away. Of course it was probably the perfect opportunity for him to grab a hotel room with one of his many ladies, as he tended to do when I was cramping his style. But for the first time in a long time, I felt like I had some freedom. Freedom and a relaxed mind. But my insomnia continued to rage on. But get this, that's not what got him expelled.

People like Dustin don't realize that eventually what you do will come back to haunt you. What goes around comes around. You reap what you sow. And that's exactly what happened to him. I mean, he didn't get wasted by another gang or anything. But he did something wrong and had to pay the consequences. He sneaked a girl in our room one night while I slept over my grandparents'. He didn't count on a random midnight room inspection by Mrs. Davis. She knocked on the door several times because she heard voices moaning erotically. But she never got a reply. So she entered with her master key. Her eyes lit up in shock, and she nodded her head in disapproval.

A female was in the midst of bouncing around the room trying to collect her bra and panties. And Dustin just stood there looking as dumb as he was for trying to pull off such a stupid stunt. Mrs. Davis went off on him. She was so loud the entire dorm could hear her. Maybe the entire campus. But even though she was loud, she did it with a dignified ease. She eventually ended her screams with the promise of a prayer for Dustin and his female companion. That's the type of person she was. Even if you were in the wrong, she'd still pray for you. And more so. Because a person in the wrong needs prayer the most. That was her philosophy.

# CHAPTER 10

# "YOU'RE NOT SPIKE LEE YET"

I'VE ALWAYS BEEN A recluse. Since childhood. And my late teenhood was pretty much the same. I went to class. Then back to my room. The only other destination I might head to was my grandparents' place. And that was constant. The more I could stay away from campus, the better. As often as I could, I got out of dodge. I moved so quickly that if you blinked, you might have missed me. Seriously. I walked fast. With my head held low. Staring at the cracks in the sidewalk. Staring at the imprints of hands in the cement ground. Some say that when a person does that, it means that they lack self-esteem and confidence. That they have problems socializing.

I admit that I might have socialization issues. But only in the sense that I'd prefer not to be distracted when I'm on a mission. If I get the vibe that a group or a person is bad news, I keep on going. And if I can help it, I just try to avoid them in the first place. I wasn't at all popular. I've never been. Matter of fact in high school, I had teachers and fellow peers that hated me. Hated me! The minute I walked in, I felt the resistance. Teachers often called me out in class just because they knew I was going somewhere in life. And don't get me started on my middle name.

Adam S. Hinson. That's my name. But no one ever thinks about the middle name, do they? No. And when you try to stress to them how important your middle name is to you, they laugh it off, ignore, or just forget. I'm sorry. But if my mother and father decided to give me a middle name, I find it hard to swallow that they did so just to do so. Why give people names they're never going to use? Use them. At least the initial. Adam S. Hinson. The 'S' stands for Scott. I think it derives from the Scotsman or something. I have to admit, the fact that my parents gave me a middle name is not the only reason why I'm so adamant about people using it. It's also because it gives me an iota of higher importance. When you have a middle name, think of how people react to you. Think of how it makes you sound. Think of how it makes you look. It makes you look like somebody. All the greats have middle names or initials. Like J. Whyatt Mondesire, Zora Neale Hurston, William H. Cosby, Samuel L. Jackson, Cecil B. Moore, Martin Luther King, Henry Louis Gates, Jr., etc.

What really eats me is that people don't always respect the middle name factor. And what makes my middle name even more important to me, is that it's my identity. My dad has the same name that I do. Adam Hinson. But there's no Junior or II in my name. I don't want that. I want my own identity. That's what's important to me. The only thing that distinguishes me from him is the 'S'. I don't have anything against my dad. He's not really in my life right now. But that's okay. I don't resent him. I'm just a separate person from him. And my middle name represents that. I've always made a big deal about my middle name. People tend to find that amusing. But I'm serious. The folks at my school wouldn't even list my name right on my school records. They claimed they were technically unable to do that. But there's got to be a way. And if there's not, they ought to figure out a way. If a person wants to use their full God-given name, they should be allowed. It should be an American right. Pander College couldn't or wouldn't even print my name properly on my identification badge. If a college president can print her full name, then why can't I?

I know what you're thinking. You're thinking I'm blowing things way out of proportion with this name thing, right? Maybe so. But it's my name. Not yours. Not anyone else's. If a person asked me to call them: 'Tissue' or 'Lizard', then I would. Why? Because that's what they desire to be called. And we're not even talking about a fake name or a nickname here in my case. We're talking about my legal middle name. But even my high school history teacher had it in for me. I signed the roll book and of course I put my middle initial. Mr. Blocker had a very public response to that at the beginning of class one day.

"S, huh?" he grumbled. "You're not Spike Lee yet."

And of course he was referring to the fact that I aspire to be a hot mainstream film director. It was quite inappropriate. A comment I shall never forget. Because I knew he wasn't saying it in jest. He meant what he spoke. It was sarcastic and spiteful. And it's a shame. Here I was at a performing arts school. A place that was supposed to be full of creativity and talent. Yet, not just students, but teachers, too, were envious of one's achievements. Again I should mention that I wasn't popular. But I had accomplished a lot at a young age. I had accomplished more than some forty year olds. And maybe I had accomplished more than Mr. Blocker, I don't know. But that was no reason for him to treat me the way he did, especially in front of the entire class. He should have embraced my talent, and helped me hone it even further. For his own benefit, he might one day have been able to say: 'I had a hand in making Adam who he is today.' But he can't say that. Not too many people can.

Mrs. Davis can say that. She wasn't just a dorm mother. She was a poet. She was a spiritual person. She was a friend. She loved to make life more exciting for students, even if it was just for the time they lived in their temporary residences. She realized that we each came from a different background, a different family, and a different style of life. But she never made anyone feel less than what they were. If anything, she boosted people's spirits as often as she could. And being that we were all freshmen in a strange place and feeling homesick, she wanted to make Chesterfield Hall feel as much like home as possible. I'd be lying if I said I wasn't homesick then. I was homesick from the moment I set foot on campus. But she really tried hard to make it easier on us. Some of the guys appreciated her. Some didn't, and that was unfortunate. But she was truly one of a kind.

Mrs. Davis would hold poetry nights and let whoever wanted to share their work do so. Dustin performed a few times prior to his expulsion. And I performed once or twice. But I only went a few times. I tried to stay away from campus, remember? She even did some of her own work from time to time. Very impressive. She invited all the dorms to come over and listen in the lobby. The crowds were never huge, but there was always a respectable number. Anyway, she knew that I lived on the computer. Whenever she'd come to spot check our room, she'd always find my eyes glued to the computer screen and my fingers glued to the keypad. So she'd always ask for me to design and print the event invitations, programs, and signs. And most importantly, she never forgot my 'S'.

But kind treatment wasn't enough to make me want to stay there. I had to flee. Anytime someone literally smiles and leaps to their feet at the opportunity to leave a place for just seconds in a day, it usually means they can't possibly belong there. I was so tired of people instructing me to give it a chance. It had been a year. I'd given it all I could. I had to go. I had to go now. Yes, I'd miss Mrs. Davis. And perhaps, I'd miss the home like atmosphere, but I was severely uncomfortable. And I had to do something about it. I made it clear to my folks that we had to find a new option for me. They weren't happy. Especially my grandparents. I think I may have driven Mom-Mom to tears, but she'd never admit it. Mom-Mom and Pop-Pop were so happy to have me close to them. Of course I was bitten by the rat of guilt. But I didn't know what else I could do. And I didn't have a license. So I didn't think it was fair to have my grandparents chauffeuring me back and forth to campus every day since I hardly stayed in my room.

"I can't say that I'm surprised." Mrs. Davis told me, upon learning of my decision to transfer. "But I sure am sorry to see ya go, ya hear? We need more students like ya around here. But if this isn't the place for ya, you're right. Ya need to be somewhere where you can be challenged. And if ya don't feel that this is the place, then I wish ya luck. But you've got to promise me one thing now, ya hear?"

"What's that?" I responded.

"That ya call me sometime. Write a letter. Come visit. Let me know how you're doing, okay?"

"For sure."

And then we hugged. A long hug. I felt like I had gained a fourth mother. There was my mom. My grandmother, Mom-Mom. And my father's mother, who lived in Brooklyn. Now I had four of them. That hug marked the end of an era. My time at Pander had come and gone. But this was just the start of my struggles in higher education.

# CHAPTER 11

# "WHITE PEOPLE!"

WHITE PEOPLE! WHITE PEOPLE! White people everywhere. My family and I were slowly cruising through this new neighborhood. Past beautiful, colorful houses with picket fences and freshly mowed lawns. Lots of people sitting on their porches and stoops. Staring at us as if we didn't belong. Glances that was reminiscent of the Jim Crow days. Naturally, I wasn't around to experience those days. But my grandparents were. And I could imagine that the treatment I was receiving at that moment was much like what happened in yesteryear. Some individuals we passed were bold enough to even nod their heads frowningly. They didn't want us here. They didn't want me here. And we were in the boondocks. The middle of nowhere. A woodsy town. A town woodsy enough for someone like me to get lost in, and never be found. I made the decision then that I would never go anywhere alone. And if I was with someone else, there had to be another minority along for the ride. And that I wouldn't drink from soda cans and glasses that I left alone momentarily, while I relieved myself in the lavatory. That I'd think twice before biting into a brownie. Call it paranoid if you'd like. But I was being cautious. It was really one of my first times experiencing racism head on.

I'm sure I experienced it beforehand. But I just didn't realize it. I had been raised in a world where color didn't matter. My mother made it clear to me that I was no different than anyone else. Don't get me wrong however. She did explain that people despised other people solely because of their skin color. And I watched movies. And I often saw how Hollywood worked. It was, and continues to be rare that a person of color is recognized by awards shows for their contribution to the industry. And it isn't satisfactory that there are only 'token blacks' on our favorite TV programs. Why aren't we headlining them? And the ones that we do headline, why are they always set in the hood? Why are we always urban or ghetto? Why are we always characters that are dysfunctional? Why are our storylines typically built around our race? Why aren't we quality characters in a quality environment, coping with quality drama? And if our race is integral, then why aren't we making issues that affect us resonate with audiences? Why are we only fleeting successes? Why are we only on certain networks? What about the big three networks. Where are we there?

And what about the stage? Why aren't more of us winning Tony Awards? Why aren't more of us on Broadway in more than just chorus parts? Why aren't we the stars? Why aren't production companies hiring minorities based on their skill and not just because of affirmative action? Why aren't we writing more screen and stage-plays? Why aren't we writing the next great American novels? Why aren't we the owners of five star restaurants and five star hotels? Why aren't we millionaires? Why aren't we executives? Why aren't we alive? Why are we dead? Why do we have lesions gracing every inch of our skin? Why are we dead? Why are we bedridden with the letters: 'H.I.V.' tattooed across our chests? Why are we dead? Why? Why are we dead?

And I read magazine and newspaper articles. And looked at photographs. And I heard stories from my grandparents. Pop-Pop couldn't sit in certain restaurants. Had to use backroom toilets. Drink from separate water fountains. Mom-Mom prayed for Dr. King on a regular basis, as well as for herself and her children. And as a kid, and a young man, I was in the center of racism and didn't even see it. But now I recall. Countless times I went to the stores in my hometown. Stores run by Caucasians, Arabs, Indians, Asians or other. And as I perused the shelves and aisles, there were eyes upon me. Every move I made was simultaneous with the moves of another. They weren't even inconspicuous about it. They blatantly followed me. Watching. Waiting. Waiting for me to discreetly snatch a candy bar and place it in my jacket. And for those of them who weren't following me, the ones who stayed behind the counter, do you know what they were doing? They were either securing the glass partitions (so many places are now famous for having, so in the event they get shot at, they'll be protected), or preparing their shotguns for possible discharge.

And in all of these cases, their behavior was based solely on assumption. They judged me. But they didn't know me. I didn't even look like the common criminal. I just looked black. And that's all they needed to see. If I looked like a duck, then chances were, I quacked. But I didn't wear baggy jeans or a long tee. I wore jeans that were fitted, a button down collar, and shoes that were shined. My typical casual/preppy dress. The same style I had when I was a kid. Of course it's evolved with the times, but the gist of my comfort level when it comes to my clothes, is pretty much the same. I'd wear a tie and vest in high school. Don't particularly like ties too much anymore. And vests are relatively outdated now. But styles change so often. And I've never been one to follow the styles. I make up my own. And that's one thing that most people don't get. That's what they don't understand about me. I might wear different pairs of socks. Sometimes they're the same color. Sometimes they're different colors. I might wear jeans with loafers. I might wear a suit pants with a jeans jacket. I don't wear clothes to tickle other people's fancies. I wear them because I want to. Obviously, I like to have a certain look. You know, that Hollywood look. But I think the

Hollywood look is basically looking unique. What's the point of looking like every other Jane and John, or Ayesha and Ahmad? I aim to be myself, plain and simple.

I could see why those folks would think I was about to steal something if I had on a wife-beater. And if I had an Afro that looked dirty with a pick sticking out of the side of it. And if my facial hair was starting to make me resemble 'Cousin It'. And if I kept my hand on the side of my pants as if I had a piece there. And if my face was permanently fixed in the form of a frown. And if a toothpick was sticking between my lips. And if precipitation was dripping from my forehead. And if the pits of my shirt were soiled. And if my disposition was that of standoffish or hostile. And if a cell phone or pager was clipped to my belt. And if my boys were sitting in front of a car parked right in front of the store, looking like they were up to something no good. But I assure you, that wasn't the case. I was dressed neat. Primped to perfection in fact. I was by myself. And all I wanted was a carton of milk and a Pepsi for my mother.

The neighborhood surrounding the campus of this new institution seemed to be quite like my childhood experiences. It seemed like no matter where I went, the drama just followed. Damn! Would I ever catch a break? The area seemed peaceful. Very quiet. One of those places where the sunlight was a permanent freeloader. Even when the clouds were angry and played bumper cars. Even when the lightning struck. Even when the moon illuminated the evening it seemed like the sun still had a place. But the cheeriness of the climate didn't erase the impoliteness of the locals. I hoped with every fiber of my being that I would not encounter the same at school itself.

Winter University. What a name. Winter is white, get it? Anyway, the school was predominately Caucasian. But there were a few minorities. Blacks, Latinos, and Asians. And you know what? The place wasn't as brutal as I expected it to be. The attitude of the neighbors didn't really trickle into the student body itself. I'm sure there were those who wished people who were dipped into chocolate sauce weren't in the same vicinity. But they weren't very vocal about it. At least not with me. And if they had something against me, they must have kept it to themselves. And the President of the school was probably one of the nicest people I've ever met. I didn't live with him. I didn't see what he did at 6pm when he departed his big office at the Administration Headquarters. But he seemed very cool, down to earth.

From the minute I set foot on the campus, the President introduced himself to me and my family. He talked a mile a minute about all the school had to offer. He was an older gentleman. Maybe sixty-something with grayish hair and funny little triangular spectacles. He smelled of Old Spice and was about five feet something. And he was white. One might argue that he only distributed such courteous salutations because I was new and it was the beginning of a new semester. But in this particular case nothing could be further from the truth. This behavior of his went on forever. He wasn't the type of school administrator who's like the great and powerful Oz, whom you never see. He wasn't like the voice of 'Charlie' whom the 'Angels' could only hear. He didn't smell of marshmallows hinting the presence of a good warlock or wizard. He made himself available to the students at all times. His office door was always open. If for some reason he was absent (whether to have a meeting, or ascertain additional school funding), students could always speak to his office administrator. And she was always in direct contact with him.

The President was the gentlest, kind, warm, and compassionate person one could meet. He really made me feel at home at Winter. I think he could tell that I was unsure of my surroundings. But he comforted me as best he could. Upon learning that my field was filmmaking and writing, he immediately informed me that I should interview with the staff of the student newspaper, The Winter Report. It was an award-winning publication that rivaled some of the student newspapers at Harvard, Princeton and the like. He didn't mention the film studies classes. But at least he gave me a start at having some happiness in my world of doom. The only reason why that place became my second choice of higher education was because my Aunt Rochelle had heard of it. She only lived about eighty miles outside of this little town. The name of the town was called Tuggsville. Tuggsville, North Carolina. Population: 4,000 or something like that.

# CHAPTER 12

# "STABBED BY FRIENDS"

MY ROOM WAS LIKE no other. It wasn't even a room. It was a suite. A spacious suite with a shower and toilet that separated my room from another. Two guys to each room. Large windows that allowed the sunlight to pour in. Sunlight was important. Especially for an artist like myself. Sunlight is my muse. Sunlight is my energy pill. The large fluorescent lighting fixtures on the ceiling were the brightest lights I've ever seen, except for the lights they use on film sets to make it look like daytime during the night. Man, the heat that those fixtures put out. Phew wee! You could literally fry a carton of eggs on that thing. The place was clean as a hospital. It even looked like a hospital. Pure white walls. It didn't smell like one, thank God. It smelled good. And it was quiet enough to hear a pin drop. And not just during the first few weeks of class. No, Carver

Hall was a library all the time. Yet people still managed to find their fun. The guys listened to their radios and CD players, but somehow managed to respect the other 100+ dorm mates.

The only minor annoyance I encountered pretty regularly was my neighbor across the hall, Chandler Serrie. He was a white kid with a bald head. Looked like a skinhead. And of course that was kind of a turnoff for me at first. At first glance, he really didn't seem like the type of person I could associate with. But he'd come to the room all the time. Actually, he had a schedule. Every Tuesday and Thursday at 6:30pm, he'd come by dressed in a suit and tie. A bible underneath his arm. He'd always give the biggest grin in the world. The grin was enough to make me wonder sometimes. But it was an innocent grin. A grin that was on his face in the event his invitation was to be accepted by me. He was sure of himself every time. He just knew that the next time would be the time I'd say yes.

"Hey, dude." Chandler would say, "Are you a Christian?"

And each time he'd begin the conversation by giving that inquiry. And each time I'd say: "Yup." But that never stopped him from asking again. One day I asked him why he'd repeatedly ask a question he already received an answer to.

"Simple." he replied, "Christian today, but just a sinner tomorrow."

"Pardon?" I said.

"We always think we have our road map together. You know? We always think that the GPS system in our ride is gonna get us to our destination. But a map was drawn up by a human, right?"

"Right."

"Okay. And a global positioning system is technology, right?"

"Right."

"Well, the thing about technology is that technology is never the same twice."

"You're losing me a little bit, Chandler."

"Okay, let me break it down like this. Technology is ever evolving, right? I mean, it's been evolving for years. We started out with computers that were the size of parking lots or whatever. Now we've got computers that are literally the size of a piece of our fingernail."

"Okay, I'm beginning to understand now."

"So what I'm saying is, you could answer 'yes' to my question now. And maybe you'd be telling the truth. I'd never assume you were lying. But even if you said 'yes', you could go home tonight and wake up tomorrow feeling different."

I guess what he was telling me was that I might say I'm a Christian. But if I don't do or say Christian things, then am I really a Christian? He didn't know what my life was like. What kind of church background I had. But he wanted to make sure that I never felt alone. And that was special. And he did it out of the kindness of his own heart. There were a lot of people like him, this being a Christian based institution. But out of the

71

many students that attended, he was the only person who treated me like a friend right off the bat. A friend. My first friend at this place. Because at the last place, I had no one. And at this place it seemed like I'd have no one. But though he was a friend, he was more like a friendly associate. I have this thing about friendship. It's part of the reason why people consider me hard to figure out sometimes.

I've got classes. There are friends. There are friendly associates. There are colleagues. There are lovers. Soul mates. Best friends. And friends on the cusp. People in my circle of association always get a kick out of the latter one. Not everyone is the type of friend I'd go out with to the cinema on the weekend. Not everyone is the type of friend I'd kiss passionately under the stars. Not everyone is the type of friend I'd lean my head on when I need to cry. Not everyone is the type of friend I'd tell my deepest darkest fears and secrets to. Not everyone is the type of friend I'd be completely honest with. There are classes. I've got classes. And I think that the people who can truly call themselves my friends, are the people that understand why I have classes. They're the people who can wait until I'm able to establish some level of trust. Because for me, trusting others is incredibly difficult.

As a young person, I was stabbed in the back so many times. Stabbed by folks who called me 'friend'. Stabbed by folks whom I called 'friend'. And though I don't sit around thinking about it all the time, I still can't forget it. I won't ever forget it. It may not have been traumatizing. But it certainly was one of those nasty scars that you get as a kid that never go away. Those scars are there to remind you of what happened. To remind you of how you felt during the event. To remind you of what you did during the event. To remind you of what you did after the event. To remind you of who you are. And to help reinforce who you are. I've come a long way since then. I've changed. And I hope to the heavens above that my backstabbers have changed. But if they haven't, that's okay. It was only a chapter in a book. But there's only one chapter in a book that never truly ends. And that's the last one.

I don't think Chandler and I could have ever been best buds. It just wasn't in the cards. But he was cool people. And that's all that mattered to me. If I needed someone to talk to, he was a door away. And vice-versa. But during the times I felt needy, I didn't talk to him. I talked to God. I'm not trying to get religious or anything. But God doesn't judge. He listens better than any friend I know. And though it may not seem like he talks back, he does. He talks loud. It's just that sometimes we drown out his voice with our own, the voice of another, or the voice of God's enemy.

# CHAPTER 13

# "WHEN THE LADY IS A BUG"

MOM-MOM HAS ALWAYS SAID that I sometimes act like a sissy. I can't help it if I don't like critters. I don't like spiders. I don't like snakes. I don't like caterpillars. When I was a kid, my grandparents would have me help them pick tobacco in the South Carolina fields. And there'd be these gross green worms that would crawl all over me. They were the same color as the tobacco leaves. So I couldn't even see that they were there. But when they'd get on my shirt and on my body, I couldn't take it. It just gave me the creeps. And even after I double checked to make sure that I was critter free, I'd still have the shakes. I'd be itching all over.

I don't like mice. I don't like rats. I don't like roaches. I don't like waterbugs or flying roaches. I don't like flying ants. I don't like bees. I especially don't like bees. If I get stung, I'll blow up. I'll blow up just like a fish. I don't like ladybugs. I don't like lightning bugs. I don't like moths. Butterflies are okay. I don't like slugs. I don't like snails. I don't like locusts. I don't like mosquitoes. I don't like bats. I don't like lizards. I don't like ferrets. Hamsters I can deal with. I don't like all the undiscovered insects that tend to roam the southern states. It's as if every time I turned around, I saw a new critter that I'd never seen before. And did I mention that I don't like ladybugs? Mom-Mom says that ladybugs are beautiful. I don't disagree. But when you're the victim of a ladybug infestation, your perspective might be slightly altered.

My room was usually super, super bright, remember? Suddenly somewhere halfway through the semester that changed. My room became dark. Very dark. The light used to reflect as white light. But now it was just black. The entire light was covered in red balls with wings. That's right. Ladybugs. Ladybugs. Ladybugs. Ladybugs everywhere. Not just there. On the windows. On the windowsill. On my dresser. In my dresser. In my closet. In my shirts and pants pockets. In my bed. My bed! My place of solace and tranquility. There aren't many young men who wouldn't enjoy a lady in their bed at some point in life. But when the lady is a bug, that could be an issue. I'd awaken in the middle of the night jumping out of bed, and stripping down to my bare skin. Ladybugs were in my boxers. And in my hair. It was driving me bananas.

I was constantly contacting the school custodial department to come out and exterminate. And they did.

But whatever they were spraying it must not have been working. It smelled horrible. They made my roommate and I vacate the premises for a couple hours while they did whatever it is they did. And this seemed to be happening often. Frequently. Constantly. Weekly. Every Tuesday it seemed. But they shouldn't have had to spray that much. It seemed like they'd spray on Tuesday. The ladybugs would die out by Wednesday or Thursday. And by the weekend they were back in full force and then some. Having lots of babies in my room. On my bed! I couldn't even sleep at night. I still had insomnia. But I couldn't sleep at all. At least when I had insomnia, I was able to fall off by around 2am. These pests made it impossible. As I laid there in bed, all I could hear was the sound of buzzing red balls. And all I could see were the miniature shadows of these balls flying and flying and flying. It seemed like they were circling me. Like some sort of ritual. Like something out of 'Exorcist' or 'Poltergeist' or something.

I had to think of an alternative to deal with this problem. I couldn't take one more moment of this insanity. So I decided to go to work. Oh yeah, did I forget to mention? I ended up getting a job as Features/Entertainment Reporter at the school paper. I never did get a byline. Well, I did. But never by myself. Every story the editor had me do, it seemed like whatever I wrote was never good enough for them. So the editor always re-wrote my stuff and I had to share the byline with her. And of course her name went before mine. I even managed to snag this big interview with one of the actors from 'Passions'. That was this weird and crazy sexy soap opera. Yes, I admit it. I watched soap operas. Still do. Blame my aunt. Not Rochelle. My other aunt. My Aunt Vanessa. She's my mom's other sister.

My Aunt Vanessa got me addicted to soaps when I was a little kid. My very first soap was 'Guiding Light'. That's what also got me addicted to the gorgeous Nia Long. Anyway, I can name all the soaps that had a hold over me for quite some time. 'The City', 'Loving', 'All My Children', 'Sunset Beach', 'One Life To Live', 'General Hospital' and of course 'Passions'. It's not really too accepted for guys to be into soaps. But there are just as many beautiful scantily clad women gracing the small screen as there are men. And that's not even why I watch them. I really watch because television is not only my refuge, television is my research. Television is my classroom. It's where I learn to write. It's where I learn to act. It's where I learn to direct. Everything I know about this business is because I watch, I do, and I read. The hours that I spend in Barnes & Noble and Borders just researching, it might just baffle you. How can anyone sit for hours and hours and just read? And take notes? And read? And take notes? It's rather simple actually. If one is passionate about what they do, it's a breeze. That's who I've always been. Someone passionate about what they do, and what they aspire to do.

The editor at the paper thought that if she published an interview with a daytime drama star, it would be blasphemous. Blasphemous because soaps are famous for depicting infidelity and baby mama drama. But I wouldn't be so quick to accuse soap operas of glorifying such things. If anything they show how horrible the aftermath of such events can be. They show how a family can be torn apart by one bad apple. But the folks at my school were too concerned that it would be improper for this interview to go to press. I fought them tooth and nail. But I lost. So I took it with a grain of salt and forged ahead. I eventually got the piece published in the local newspaper, which ultimately was a bigger venue anyway. Yay!

I wasn't really getting everything that I wanted to out of this job. I wanted to write stories that would get me noticed. That would get me gigs at 'The New Yorker' and 'The New York Times', or 'The Hollywood Reporter'. I wanted to write stories that would be so interesting that people would be calling to interview me. I wanted to write stories that would help change the world just a little bit, one step at a time. Kind of idealistic, I know. But it can happen. Change can happen. So I had to make the best out of the situation I was in. I wasn't really able to concentrate on my film studies like I anticipated, so this was the next best thing.

Before I came to Winter, I was under the impression they had a film studies department. I was erroneously informed that there were cameras and editing equipment. But in reality, all that existed were two classes and they were both film theory. Film theory is great, but what good is theory without being a part of making an actual film? The only way that I was able to even partly satisfy myself was by continuing to make my own shoestring budgeted projects. And continuing to enter them into as many festivals and showcases as I possibly could. It was tough. And I had some modest success. Not nearly as much as I'd have liked. But I had to make what I could out of what I had. And that was usually very little. The entry fees were mad crazy. The more festivals a filmmaker is in, the better chance he has at being noticed.

The only person that seemed to notice me was my room mate. His name was Kenny. Kenny Jung. He was a Korean guy.

———◆◆◆◆◆———

# CHAPTER 14

# "DO YOU PEOPLE TAKE SHOWER?"

IT WASN'T HIS FULL name. It wasn't his native name. Kenny was his American name. His real name I couldn't pronounce or spell if I wanted to. It's one of those names you'd expect to find in a spelling bee competition. Like a hundred different letters or something, you know?

Kenny, for some reason, thought I was a celebrity. I guess it had something to do with all the paraphernalia I had plastered all over my walls. My articles. Articles written by me. Articles written about me. Photographs, headshots. Quotes about me from famous folks. Movie posters. You get it. And I had all these things there to add to my sunlight. Because I feel that an artist can always have more than just one muse. My previous work is my muse. Because what I've done in the past makes me want to surpass it. Outdoing others is fine and dandy. It might even be fun. Especially if you're the type to get your rocks off on making others swoon at your success, and wallow over the lack of their own. I'm not one of those folks, by the way. But if it's in my face all the time that I've got to continue to work as hard as I possibly can, then that's what I'm going to do. And that's exactly what my 'Wall of Shame' did for me.

Kenny knew I was a Philly boy. But he kept telling all his friends that I made the movie, 'Philadelphia'. Now as flattering as that was, especially since it's one of my favorites, I couldn't take credit for that. That was a feat of John Demme. But Kenny still wouldn't believe it. And all the friends he told were always Korean like him. I'm not sure if they were new to America and didn't realize who was who. But why didn't they realize that if I was some famous hotshot film producer, I probably wouldn't be sitting in a dorm room at a college in the middle of nowhere? At first I thought he was kidding. Just making conversation. Being sarcastic. But these comments never stopped. So after awhile, I just let it go. If he and his friends wanted to idolize me or whatever, great. I wouldn't complain. Especially since his friends were always females.

Usually three of them. He'd always have three ladies visit him. One of them was kind of cute. The other two weren't my type. They'd visit often. I could tell the relationships between all four were strictly platonic. But the cute one wasn't looking my way either. Not that I was trying to holler at her. My time was still royally compromised. But a person would be lying if they said they'd never want to experience being admired by someone. It felt good. It felt great. These ladies never got on my nerves, but they were in my room all the time for this guy. Thankfully he didn't use the room as a lobby where the whole world could come to wait, play and do whatever.

Maybe the ladies came all the time because Kenny was sort of a jock. If they considered golf to be the 'jock' type sport. Kenny was a golf prodigy. At Winter on scholarship straight from his homeland. The grapevine gossiped that he never lost a game, that Winter was lucky to have him. I think he was a junior. He was tall with dark straight hair. High-pitched voice, but not like a girl. Just higher than normal. And he ate, breathed, and slept all things golf. Parallel to my world of film obsession, his wall was covered in golf paraphernalia. Clippings of the greats including Tiger Woods. Kenny adored that man and said it was he who made him a better golfer.

Kenny and I got along pretty well. He seemed like a nice guy. I could understand him, but I had to ask him to repeat himself a lot. Especially since I was the only one that had to deal with him speaking in *my* native tongue. He only spoke English to me really. The rest of the time he was speaking his language into the phone, or to his friends. Sometimes it bothered me a little. I'd get a little paranoid that maybe he was making fun of me or something. But that was ridiculous. I don't think he was thinking about me at all. Except there were a few times when a few English words would slip out while he was on the phone. And those English words were: 'Adam', 'Philadelphia', 'Famous filmmaker', etc. Again it was flattering. But embarrassing, too.

When Kenny found out I was a writer, and that I had received an 'A' and a 'B' in my English classes, he requested that I'd help him out.

"What do you need help with?" I asked him.

"I speak English not too good." he said, "And I have to write paper for English class. I got 'D' on last paper. Can you help me?"

"Yeah, I guess I can do that."

So I wrote papers for him week after week. Let me correct myself. I didn't actually write them. But I'd take what he wrote and edit it. Make it sound better. Just add some pizzazz here and there. Sometimes I wouldn't go to sleep because I'd be so into whatever my mind was creating, I couldn't close my eyes. And it's not even like the paper was my own. I was just expanding on his ideas, which were written with no punctuation and no real structure of sentences. But everything I did for Kenny would eventually mean nothing.

One evening, I was sitting on my bed scanning the pages of a novel. Kenny walked in and initiated a conversation that would change the entire dynamic of our relationship. But he didn't ask it straight off. He must have been thinking about how he was going to pose the inquiry. Because he seemed to be idly moving about the room. Shuffling items on his desk for no apparent reason. Eventually he sat down on his bed, and turned to me.

"Hey, can I ask you question?" he said, softly.

"Go head." I replied, resting my novel in my lap.

"Do you guys take shower?"

"Pardon?"

"Do you take shower?"

"Didn't you just see me come out of the shower this morning?"

"It's just, I heard you guys don't like to take shower."

"Why wouldn't we want to take showers?"

"You don't want hair to get wet."

I grinned. And not a happy one either. Firstly, the words 'you guys' totally threw me for a loop. After two months of being roomies, he now suddenly decides to spurt racial epithets at me? That was the end of the 'cordial' me. I may have always been an Aquarius minded individual, meaning I spoke when I needed to. But I still tried to be tight lipped as much as I could. But he pressed a button that evening that he shouldn't have pressed. I wasn't sure if he meant to do it, or if it was a Freudian slip. But he did it. And frankly, he should have known better.

"Who told you that we don't like to take showers?" I asked him, with a stern lip, a twitching eye, and balled fists. And I was standing up at this point. The minute he said what he said, I was standing up. I leaped up like a frog. A frog who had an identity crisis and thought he was a lion about to devour his prey. Because believe me, I was ready to do just that. But I was trying to hold composure. I was trying to be civil. Handle things as quietly as possible. I didn't want to be expelled from school for violence. But I couldn't just stand, be still, and be silent. Oh no, not I.

What began as a conversation quickly ensued into an argument. I was in his face. You know how brothas used to be all up in each other's territory? Face to face? Cheek to cheek? Lips inches apart from each other? And rage in both of their eyes? Looking like they were about to kiss? But in reality, they were about to kill each other? Or at least try? That's how Kenny and I were. I wasn't a fighter. I don't like blood. I can write about it. I can make movies about it. But when it's real, I can't stand it. I shouted at him from the top of my lungs. He shouted back. He claimed he didn't know what he said was wrong. Bullshit! Don't patronize me.

Our altercation ruined every bit of silent ecstasy that this dorm had. We must have awakened the dead with our voices. Kenny was trying to come off as a hard dude. But it wasn't scaring me. He wasn't scaring me at all. I think I might have actually scared *him* a little. He probably never expected to see me go ballistic on him. But I didn't have a choice. He drove me to it. I was nothing but good to him. I even gave him boxes of Tastykake as a kind gesture. They weren't available in every area of the south. And him being a newcomer to this country, it was the first time he ever heard of it. But he loved biting into every morsel of pound cake. But now he was treating me like this?

The Resident Advisors, both of them, knocked on the door. Things were so loud that people were probably under the impression the two of us were beating the crap out of each other. I answered the door.

"Is everything okay here, guys?" said one of the R.A.s.

"My room mate is a racist." I snapped.

"No, I not." Kenny protested.

Then the other R.A. asked me to step outside into the hallway so his partner could talk to my room mate. I refused. I told them that I didn't instigate the situation, and therefore I shouldn't have to go out into the hall. It dawned on me that I was in the midst of people who didn't look like me. I was outnumbered. It was no surprise that they thought I started all the trouble. Always the Negro, right? The Resident Advisors suggested that I consider relocating to another room. So as to avoid any further conflict. Why was this suggested to me and not to Kenny? I refused. Once again they pointed the finger of guilt at me. And once again, I stood my ground. I told them that I wasn't going anywhere.

If they wanted a resolution to the problem, then Kenny needed to go. They asked Kenny if he indeed said what I accused him of saying. By this time, he couldn't deny. Why would I make up something so serious? Especially since I was the quiet kid. Yet even though it was perfectly clear I was not in the wrong, the R.A.s still did everything in their power to try and make me feel and look guilty. But my people have been persecuted and prosecuted for things they simply did not do for lifetimes. I wasn't going to allow this instance to be added to the statistics list of injustices to the minority.

I looked each R.A. in the eye for a few moments. Assuring them that their attempt at being intimidating forces was not a threat to me. I then looked Kenny in the eye. And my glance at him was dripping fury. I walked over to my bed and sat down. I picked up my novel, reopened it, and my eyes began to scan the pages for a second time that day. I needed to get away. And I hoped my book would take me there.

# CHAPTER 15

# "FUNNY, FUNNY, FUNNY…"

I WAS GOING BECAUSE I had to. There was no guarantee that my life would be made in the shade. If there was, I might have considered putting a college education on the backburner. Since the beginning of college, I felt like all I wanted to do was get it over with. Many people say that when starting school. But I really meant it. I wanted to be working in my field. And every time an opportunity came about, I could never take it. Why? Because school seemed to be in the way. One job I'll never forget is a job I had to pass on. The folks from the 'Miss America' pageant wanted me to be a production assistant. I'm not sure if it was for the television broadcast, or just the contest itself. But it really didn't matter. I would have been in Heaven. The chance to be surrounded by sexy, beautiful women dressed in next to nothing. I wouldn't have cared if all I was doing was scrubbing the toilets in the ladies room. Just being able to gaze at eye-candy from all around the country would have been enough for me. It would have been a week long gig. And the pay wasn't awful. But I couldn't take off for classes to head to Jersey to work.

This wasn't the only gig I missed out on. I missed out on dozens. Crew work and on-screen stuff. It made me sick to my stomach that I couldn't take advantage of some of what was being offered. I was getting calls all the time. That's why I made my mother make a pact with me. She wasn't allowed to tell people exactly where I was and what I was doing. Not everyone knew that I was pursuing a college education. Most naturally assumed that I had been through film school because of what I already knew. The most my mom was allowed to tell folks was that I was out of town. The majority took that to mean I was working on productions out of town or something. My mom wasn't lying. It was called being a good publicist really. You think the President is always where they say he is? Of course not. That's how he's made secret trips to Iraq and stuff right under our very noses.

My mother had to give excuses. Otherwise I'd lose out on even more work. And I didn't want everyone to think that I was unavailable period. Because that wasn't the case. It may have been difficult to miss classes for work. But if a truly great thing knocked on my door, I wouldn't have been able to resist it. My school and I would have had to make some sort of special arrangement. I'm not famous. But plenty of celebrities have gone to college while still being entertainers. Julia Stiles, The Olsen Twins, Jonathan Taylor Thomas. If the world makes provisions for them, why can't the world make provisions for me? I may be considered a 'nobody' by recognition standards. But I'm far from a 'nobody'. And this 'nobody' might just be a 'somebody' down the road. So it seemed like the school should embrace a student on his way. And Winter didn't do a bad job at that. It's just that everything I was being offered it seemed wasn't feasible at the time.

Summer had arrived. And I said goodbye to Winter, too. I know what you're thinking. You left another school? I've been doing it all my life. I went to a Montessori school from pre-school to seventh grade. But by then, I wanted to experience something new. Why I waited until the next to the final year of Montessori to decide to go somewhere else, I'm not sure. But 7th grade was a mixture of two schools. I first tried a public school in Bensalem, Pennsylvania. Stayed there for about a month and a half. But I hated it there. Part of it may have had to do with me being in unfamiliar territory. The place just seemed very cold. Not in temperature. There was just a very cold vibe. It was mandatory that I be part of the band. But I basically just sat there every day and watched the other young musicians. Because I couldn't play jack. I used to play the keys, but my music teacher at Temple got sick and moved to Australia.

My mother then came up with a bright, but crazy idea. She suggested that I relocate to an entirely different state. I was reluctant at first. But it was probably one of the best academic related decisions I've ever made in my life. I stayed with Aunt Rochelle for seventh grade. I attended Brook Junior High in Raleigh. With the exception of the usual school bullies, my time there was great. And these bullies weren't the types to actually pick fights. They were all mouth. Always taller and bigger than me. They tried to act mean. But they only came off as annoying. They'd never fail to crack jokes about my low weight, lack of muscle, and the way I dressed and spoke. I was preppy. Still am. And I talked proper. Still do. They'd also call me 'white'. They'd call me that all the time. Just because I enunciated my words and completed my sentences. There's nothing wrong with being complete, is there?

I made a few friends there. One of them was my aunt's next door neighbor. We always rode the school bus together in the mornings. And I'd have the kids on the bus rolling in laughter. I wasn't trying to be funny. Because I'm far from funny. People tell me that I'm funny because I'm not trying to be funny. So if I really am funny, I find that to be funny. But I used to tell everyone that I was an alien. And most of them believed me because I wasn't like the rest of them. I didn't have that thick rich southern accent. Anyone I came across could instantly tell that I was from the north. Maybe my accent was a thick rich northern one. I was usually quiet. And I usually kept to myself. So others found that to be strange. I wasn't really socializing with anyone else. But every now and then, I'd tell people that I was born on Jupiter and raised on Mars. Therefore, I was a

Jupiteranian Martian. I have no idea why I did that. I don't know if I was just trying to have fun. Or maybe I was trying to ignore how it felt to be in a new place yet again.

It was a miracle that they admitted me two months after the semester had already begun. If I had been enrolled and missed that many classes, I'd have been expelled. These kind folks at Brook allowed me in. And a funny thing happened to me while there. My favorite class turned out to be science. I wasn't passing the class with flying colors. But the class was interesting. We all got to spend the first fifteen minutes of class watching this high school drama show on TV called 'Degrassi'. And the first half of it, I got to watch in homeroom, since thankfully it was back to back with science. My teacher was cool. He was truly a free spirit. Crazy electrocuted grayish white hair and a moustache with curls on the sides. He made our first in class assignment be making a jug of some type of alcoholic drink.. I'm not sure if that was legal. But he told us that we'd be working on it for a few weeks. I never realized that it took so long to make an alcoholic beverage. He had all the ingredients. Yeast and apples included. It was different, his style of teaching. I wondered if when the jug of alcohol was complete, he'd be throwing it out, or taking it home to consume himself.

I enjoyed that year. I'd have to say that it was really my most memorable educational experience. But I couldn't stay for eighth grade. Living with Aunt Rochelle and her son was starting to be problematic. I loved them both. And they loved me. But people need space. And we people needed it badly. So I returned to my Montessori school for eighth grade. My old friends and teachers were overjoyed to see me again. They told me they knew I couldn't stay away. I laughed. I was happy to be back. But I could have stayed away. I could have found somewhere else to go, but this was the easiest choice. But being able to soon graduate from the school I spent my entire childhood at would mean a great deal.

I didn't know what to do with myself now that summer vacation was around. And I knew that I had to make some type of educational decision. Where was there left to go? All the summer jobs in the city pretty much had been filled. Filled by lots of eager high school and college kids wanting to make some quick bucks that summer. Then the phone rang. A friend of mine at The Pennsylvania Film Commission called. He informed me that a TV show was about to start filming in Philly. I really wanted to be a part of this action. The first major series to be shot here tanked. This was our opportunity for the city to redeem itself. And my opportunity to shine. I wasn't sure what positions were available. But the best job for me was probably production assistant, or assistant director. Even if I only worked during the summer, I was going to try with all my might to work on this production. The folks at Redial Entertainment didn't know me from Adam. But they were about to.

---

# CHAPTER 16

# "PILOT EPISODE"

MY FINGERS WERE TWIDDLING. Maybe I was a little nervous. It wasn't the first time I've had a job interview. But I really, really wanted this particular job. I sat in a large spacious office in a building on Broad and Walnut Street. Right across the street from City Hall. The crystal windows were large and wide. This allowed the sunlight to pour in. The sunlight was so pure, and the little specks from the sun were dancing on the other buildings outside. Usually the business district is dim because the skyscrapers are so tall. But the sun would not allow this parade to be rained on.

I was sitting on the guest side of a weathered presidential desk that was relatively bare, except for two laptop computers, scripts, paperwork, and schedules. A large poster for the TV series hanged behind. It read: 'Redial Entertainment Presents *The Drop*'. The show was about a brother and sister team of DEA agents. And the stars of the show were some major movie people. I sneakily perused some of the pages of the shooting script for the pilot episode. It seemed real interesting. It was a real fast read. Lots of action. Sparse dialogue. The script made it seem like this show would be an expensive one to produce.

A Latino man soon entered and took a seat behind his desk. His name was Antonio Martin. He rearranged some papers on his desk, and then opened a folder with my name printed on it. He scanned the resume during our conversation. He asked what my experience was in the business, how much professional work I've done, and what I'd be most interested in doing on this production. It turned out that there were really only three jobs that I qualified for. Production assistance, which anyone can do. No, I take that back. Anyone <u>can</u> do it. But that doesn't mean they'll do it well. And it doesn't mean they'll be able to handle the grueling reality of the job. The second job was script supervision. This wasn't an easy job at all. But I refuse to ever do that one again. I had a real bad experience on a feature film I worked on the summer before. The camera crew just didn't get along with me. Perhaps it was because I was young. Perhaps it was because I wasn't working in a manner they deemed professional. But when I got yelled at by the film loader, that was the end of it. I try to never talk back to anybody on a set in front of folks. But he called me out in front of one hundred people. I couldn't let that fly.

The third job was assistant director. Not the 'first' position. Not even the 'second' one. I was only eligible for $2^{nd}$ $2^{nd}$ Assistant Director. But Mr. Martin didn't think that role was appropriate for me because most of my professional work had been in the independent realm. That's the one thing about the entertainment business that I've always hated. You can't get a really good job unless you've had the experience. And you can't get the experience unless you've had a really good job. It's a catch 22. But it really didn't matter what job I got. As long as I was able to work on this series, it was the only thing that mattered to me. Mr. Martin informed me that he'd give me a call in a few days, and let me know what his decision was. I'm sure a production could never get enough production assistants, but he still had other candidates to interview. I stood up, shook his hand, smiled, straightened my tie, put on my shades and departed. I tried to be optimistic. But deep down I wasn't quite sure if this job was going to be mine.

Two weeks later at 7am, I was wiping my weary eyes as I approached $11^{th}$ and Walnut Street. That's where 'The Drop' was filming on that day. It was day one of production. Shooting of the pilot episode. And yours truly was officially a Set Production Assistant. I was only a smidge nervous. I had done this job several times in the past. But this was the first time I'd be working on a mainstream national television show that would be seen by the millions. I walked over to the corner where about ten trailers and various trucks were parked. The streets were roped off. Lots of passers-by were eyeballing anyone that had anything to do with the production. I stopped at the honeywagon and knocked on the door of the production hub. The door opened and a young woman with braided hair slapped a walkie-talkie in my hand. She identified herself as the Key Set Production Assistant and told me to report to the catering truck, which was two blocks down. It was later that I actually got her name. Cordiality wasn't her plan upon my arrival. It was business. Just business.

I stood at the catering truck putting on my walkie-talkie. The caterer asked if I wanted something for breakfast. The menu was a smorgasbord. Bacon, sausage, pancakes, hash browns, eggs, potatoes, waffles and too many other mouthwatering delights. But before I could place my order, I was paged over the walkie. I was told to get a bowl of hot grits and to immediately take it to the hospital entrance around the corner. That's where the filming was taking place today. And Kasey, the Key Set PA, my boss, told me to step on it. The breakfast item was for the Guest Star of the pilot episode, Jimmy Cardon. He was a hotshot producer from LA, but he was also a highly accomplished actor. I ordered the item and upon receiving it, I ran to the hospital as fast as I possibly could. Trying to make sure that nothing spilled.

I entered the hospital and was directed towards a back room by a fellow PA. I knocked on the door. After a few moments the door opened. Sitting on the floor on a pillow was Jimmy. Standing over him was the Director of the episode as well as the Director of Photography.

They were going over last minute script changes. Jimmy never looked at me. I stood for quite some time just holding his breakfast in my hand. Waiting for him to acknowledge my presence. But he never did. Kasey eventually came up behind me and grabbed the bowl out of my hand. She sternly walked right up to him and handed him the meal. He looked up at her smiled. She walked up to me and whispered into my ear.

"You've got to be assertive, Adam." she said, while leading me out.

Assertive? She didn't know the first thing about me. I'm very assertive. I've always been assertive ever since that one time when I was a toddler, and Aunt Rochelle taught me that I have the right away, and not just when it comes to crossing the street. I was five maybe. And she and I were at a supermarket in Manning, South Carolina. I put a quarter into a candy machine but when I turned the little dial, nothing happened. Nothing came out. So I put in one more quarter, but still I was without my tooth destroying sweet treat. My eyes began to water. I was upset. Aunt Rochelle walked me up to the customer service counter.

"My son lost his money in your machine." she told him. And she called me her son because it had a little more weight than if she were to have said, my nephew. She knew how to work it.

"I'm sorry, Miss." said the Manager, "I'm not in control of what happens with the machines here."

"But you manage this establishment, correct?"

"Yes, but—"

"Then that means you also manage the machines because they're in your establishment, correct?"

"Miss, I have nothing to do with that. The machines belong to outside companies. I just rent them the space."

"You just rent them the space, huh? Okay, well then give me the name and contact information of this company."

"Miss, I really am not at liberty to give out such information."

"You're not at liberty? I want your boss's name. And I want his contact information. I also want your name."

"Miss, I'm very sorry about this."

"No, you're not. We're talking about two quarters. Fifty cents. Look at that boy."

She pointed at me. Tears were streaming down my face at warp speed.

"My son is crying." she said, "Crying because he wants some bubble gum. Crying because your machine took his money and won't give it back. Either give me the information, or give me two quarters. That choice is yours."

"Okay, Miss." said the Manager, "You got it. You win."

The Manager opened the cash register and removed two quarters. He reached out his hand to give them to Aunt Rochelle. She just nodded her head and pointed to me.

"Don't give it to me." she said, cutting her eyes. "Give it to him."

The Manager paused and then did just that. Then he turned his back, humiliated. He was so stingy, that he almost didn't care if a five year old boy thought it was the end of the world because his money was lost. Things like this would happen to me repeatedly as time progressed. But because of her, I learned that I had the right away. Like this one time when my cousin and I were at Chicken World. We ordered two separate meals. One for him and the other for me. Fries and chicken. Sitting across from the counter was a very noisy family. A boisterous one, too. I assume that the parents were somewhere around. But all I could see and hear were the five rambunctious kids sitting at the table. They should have been sitting. But they were actually sitting, standing, laying, and doing everything else a kid could do on a tabletop. They were completely out of control. I thought to myself that when I have children, if they ever act like that, I'm disowning them. But seriously, the lack of home training and dining etiquette was brightly evident.

As the server reached out her hand to distribute my food, one of the kids came up and knocked my French fries to the floor. The server actually expected me to order another box of fries. She must have been on crack. She saw exactly what happened. I don't know if the kid did it accidentally, or was just being a mischievous little devil. But the server saw what the kid did. It wasn't my fault by any means. I had just spent ten bucks of my own hard earned pay (my allowance), for me and my cousin's meals. There was no way I was depleting my wallet any further. I asked to see the establishment manager, but was informed that he was unavailable. You know I didn't leave it at just that. I called the main office of Chicken World as soon as I got home. Gave them my receipt number, the name of my server, the location name since it was a chain, and the time of the event. A day later, I received a call. I was offered a meal for six anytime I wanted, completely on the house.

# CHAPTER 17

# "*STARBUCKS & THE STARS*"

I WAS ON HIATUS from school. But working on 'The Drop' wasn't easy. Not that I expected it to be. But I just never expected that I'd be stepped on as much as I was by my bosses, which really seemed to be everyone. I was reprimanded by Kasey for giving Jimmy Cardon the wrong breakfast. He asked for grits, but somehow he ended up with cream of wheat. How was I supposed to know? And why was I in the wrong? I wasn't the caterer. He should have known the difference. I was very clear when I made the request. I defended myself as best I could. But it was my first day on the job and I really didn't want to press anyone's buttons, nor did I want to press my luck. I was a new face. And I didn't want my 'assertiveness' to piss off the wrong people, or else I might have been out of a job. And Jimmy wasn't the only haughty talent I had to put up with.

At least the main stars of the show were peachy to deal with. It was these guest stars that breezed in and out that made my work life unbearable. They always had to have things their way, or no way. Their way, or the highway. On one episode the guest star was this famous woman named Telly Parker. She was tall and beautiful. But that didn't take the place of her ugly attitude. I understood that she was ill while filming, the flu I believe. But that was no reason to make the rest of us, most especially myself, feel like we had the flu, too. She requested hot chicken noodle soup and a cup of hot coffee. But not just any coffee. Starbucks coffee. I went to a convenience store near our location. I gave her the soup, but she complained that it was not only lukewarm instead of hot, it also had no taste. I couldn't get Starbucks because it was after hours. So I got her some coffee from the same store, and she had a bloody fit. She even spit it out upon sipping some. She hissed at me like a snake. At least that's what it sounded like. *Sssss.* I did what I could. She asked for something. And I delivered the best way I could. It's not my fault if the soup and the coffee weren't to her liking. Oh, didn't I mention, that I was the Coffee and Starbucks king?

I had no problem making coffee for folks. Antonio couldn't function without his coffee. And he only allowed me to prepare it. He said it was the best he ever tasted. And all I did was pour some coffee in a Styrofoam cup, drop some milk and sugar in it, and call it a day. It's not like I sat there and grinded the beans. But he trusted no one with his coffee except me. He had one in the morning. One in the afternoon. One at lunch. One at dinner. One at second meal. He only wanted my coffee when he couldn't get what all showbiz folks seem to be obsessed with. Starbucks.

Whenever the good folks at Starbucks would see me coming, they either ducked or ran. They were happy for the business because we gave them plenty. But they never had prior warning that 'The Drop' was about to invade. And many times we were turned away from one Starbucks, and sent to another because they couldn't handle our large orders. The thing that really got on my nerves was that Kasey and the rest of them always expected things to be done at the snap of a finger. But that wasn't always possible. You can't send me to Starbucks to fetch one hundred different drinks. 100! 100 in the literal sense. And all of them different. Some cold. Some hot. You can't send me to do that and then expect that when I return, every hot drink will be hot, and every cold one cold. And the rushing drove me bananas.

I was often sent to get sushi, too. And this one time I must have been phoned eight times in a matter of twenty minutes because I wasn't back yet with the order. Eventually it got to the point where it was time for everyone to meet the real Adam. I couldn't bite my tongue any longer. They made me purchase a cellular telephone so they could be in constant contact with me. Before that I never had need for a phone. These people even called me on the occasional day I decided to take a hiatus from work. I told Kasey that if the Director of Photography wanted his sushi right away, then the order should have been placed before lunch was called. I told them that if they expected me to move at Superman speed, they'd better take a reality pill.

I think most of the family there came to respect me more when they figured out that I refused to be a piece of the ground they spit on. If something was wrong, I spoke on it. We were shooting one time in an old basement of a church in South Philly. But the location was filled with asbestos. The actors had masks to wear. The above the line crew had masks to wear. But not I? And they expected me to walk into that place? I refused. Every time Kasey would yell at me over the walkie-talkie to run instead of walk, I refused.

"If I run, what good is that to you?" I told her, "Sets are dangerous places as you and I both know. There are cables, lights, and equipment. If I trip and fall and break my neck, what good is that to you? And what good does that do for me? It doesn't. I can try to walk a little faster. But I'm not running on a film set. You want me to move faster, give me some skates."

The last part of my statement was said more out of anger. But it's how I felt. And Kasey should have known better than anyone than to ask me to run. I was always the designated PA to accompany injured crew to the hospital. And there were hospital visits weekly. This was a new show. We were shooting in a city that didn't exactly meet the technical aptitude of Hollywood, New York and Canada. Chaos was constant. The LA producers were always on set making

106

it difficult for the directors and local producers to do their jobs properly. The injuries were momentous and all completely different. The sound guy slipped on the camera truck during a slick rainstorm and broke his ankle. That put him out of work for four weeks. The driver of the honeywagon got his foot caught in the lift-gate of a truck and severed a toe or two. Even Kasey herself had a major medical scare. She had a severe asthma attack one evening on set that scared the living daylights out of us all. She fell to the ground and her eyes were bugging out. They eventually rolled to the back of her head. And she was gasping and gasping. She couldn't breathe. My stomach sank.

The show's producer, a Jewish woman named Lola, understood my concerns. She became my best friend while working there. We weren't privy to that much time together, but we understood each other I believe. I think it was because we both had a similar work ethic. My other buddies, the Teamsters, couldn't understand our relationship. Because most people hated her guts. I'm not sure why. I didn't really get to see what went on behind the scenes with her. But I imagine she was a tough, no nonsense boss. And that coming from a woman can make a man feel worthless. But I admired it. She'd come to set and demand that craft service rearrange their food display and things like that. She didn't just deal with the matters of the show's business. She also wanted things to be the right way for all of us. Especially on the days when LA was in town. She was hardnosed alright, but my favorite ally.

My association with Lola I was sure would be tested after I did something I would never do again. She asked me to borrow a pen. I gave her mine. But at the end of the day, I still hadn't gotten it back. And I wanted it. I'm a writer. When I write, I have to use a certain type of pen, or else things don't feel complete. And I was always writing while on set. I kept a small notebook in my back pocket. The stars of the show would often ask what I was working on. I'd say: 'The Next Great American Screenplay'. If we were in Hollywood, that statement might not have carried much weight. Everyone there is writing one. From your cabbie to the tattoo artist on the corner. But I was in Philly. And I was a kid. A young man, but I looked like a kid. I think these screen veterans admired that.

I called the production office and asked to speak to Lola. Her personal assistant told me that she was on a conference call with LA. I left the message that I needed my pen back. I didn't realize that requesting my pen back was a major 'no-no'. But I did it anyway. And it didn't take very long for word to travel around set of what I did. Everywhere I went people were joking with me about what happened. I even got a few somber nods from people who didn't expect me to be at work tomorrow, as Lola had a penchant for getting rid of folks on a regular basis. I wasn't too worried though. I knew that Lola and I were tight. I more so felt embarrassed. But she had a good sense of humor, which was validated the next day at work, when her personal assistant came all the way to set to hand me a bag with my name written on it. I anticipated what might be inside. Kasey looked over curiously. I opened the bag to find dozens of pens and a note.

>*Dear Adam,*
>
>*I think I lost your pen. Here are some replacements.*
>
>*–Lola*

It was very nice of her to just drop the situation. And to do it in a humorous way. She could have made me sweat it out by being the tough cookie she was known for being. But she didn't. And I'll forever appreciate that. After working on the series for season one, I came to the realization that my time might be winding down there. I had accomplished what I set out to accomplish. A resume credit. The chance to network. And observe on set and off set operations. It felt excellent to actually be working in the field. And to be getting paid 500 smackaroos weekly. But I knew that a production assistant job was not my ultimate goal, I didn't want to be doing it forever. I also knew that my higher education would continue to wait in the wings until I did something about it.

# CHAPTER 18

# "THE THIRD WORLD"

I WAS NEVER SURE about attending an all black college. It just seemed to me that college was supposed to prepare you for the world. But the world is a huge place. And in it are people that are all different. So if I'm at a college where everyone looks like me, how is that really prepping me for the world? But on the flip side, I also recognized that learning more about heritage and how to associate with my people was an integral part in being a productive member of society. Growing up, I never really got told about my ancestors and even what my more recent relatives went through. The history books gave like a page or two to the minority struggle. We spent more time talking about Christopher Columbus discovering America, which there seems to be a lot of disagreement about. We spent more time talking about wars that were fought, but we never talked about how minorities played a major role in some of those battles. We never talked about the Tuskegee Airmen. We never talked about the Pullman Porters. And maybe, just maybe, the black college experience would do that for a brotha, or a sista. Maybe it would do it for me.

I was in the Third World. My third world of higher education. It took a lot to please me. I have high expectations for everyone. I have high expectations for me. The name of the college was called Readmore. It was located in Raleigh, North Carolina. And Aunt Rochelle worked there. That's how I found out about the place. When she learned that I was once again pursuing a new venue for my studies, she suggested this place. I wasn't enthusiastic. But at least I knew that if necessary, she'd have my back. The campus was small, much like the first black school I went to a couple of years ago. I arrived to the Carolinas safely. I arrived to campus safely. But actually registering for classes was a major test. A major test of my patience.

7:50am. Student Union. I was standing in a lonnnnnnnng line. A long line of about a hundred or so folks. We were waiting at the bottom of a large staircase, which lead upstairs to where the action was. But the gate was down and two security officers were standing guard. The area was roped off so as to promote an orderly line. But the ropes were so short that no one really paid them any attention. It was clear that as soon as the gate was lifted it would be a free for all. I was sixth in line, and I was trying desperately to hold my place. I was determined not to let myself get pushed to the side. I got here early so I could get my stuff in order as quickly as possible. Finally, the gate began to rise. And the crowd pushed to the front. It was eight o' clock now, and security wasn't budging.

We must have stood there in line for nearly an hour and a half. Just waiting. I was very impatient. Many people were. It was time being wasted. I couldn't understand why the ball hadn't been rolled yet. Registration was scheduled to begin at 8. Why had I gotten here early this morning if they were going to begin late? I could have slept an extra hour. During the time we waited, the Registrar passed by a few times and didn't say word one to any of us. And when some of us tried to ask her what was going on, she ignored. When security finally began letting us up it was in groups of two. Despite their keeping things together as best they could, people were still knocking others out of line. I even got shoved a few times, but I was close enough to the steps to hold onto the guardrail.

Upstairs there were chairs. Rows and rows of chairs. And these chairs were at each of the seven workstations. Each workstation had several staff and faculty members sitting behind computer screens. Stations included Registration, Financial Clearance, Housing, Advisement, etc. I had to play musical chairs with everyone. As each person was seen by a counselor we'd have to relocate to the seat next to us. Thankfully, I was number six. It didn't take long at all for me to be seen. But the process didn't end at that point. It really never began. Because I was informed that I couldn't register until my financial information was taken care of. I told them that everything was fine. My mother and I had called a few times before I even left Philly to make sure that when I arrived, all I had to do was walk in the door.

Aunt Rochelle came to the rescue. I had to call her for help. I couldn't reach my grandmother. I think she was at work. She's a teacher. I couldn't get my mom either. She's a publicist for some underground indie bands back home. And I knew nothing about my financial records and whatnot. None of the money I was spending for school was my own. It was all money that I'd eventually have to pay back. Loans and stuff. Not that my aunt knew anything about my finances because she didn't. But maybe she'd be able to at least help expedite the situation. I needed to register for my classes before they closed. I needed to move into my room before I was stuck on a side that I'd prefer not to be. I used to be reluctant when coming to a new place. But this time around all I wanted to do was get it over with. The sooner I could move into the dorm, the sooner I could start classes. The sooner I could start classes, the sooner I'd be on track to finish classes.

My aunt walked over with me to the Financial Aid office on the east side of campus. It was a four minute walk. But the walk seemed longer. Everywhere my aunt went, people stopped to say hello. It was like one big family so it wasn't unnatural that she often had to stop to greet people. But it was a non-stop thing. And it wasn't just like this on campus. It seemed like no matter where my aunt and I went, people knew her. In the supermarket. At the dollar store. At the gas station. It never failed. As we walked, people said: 'Good morning' to me. I up-ticked my head. But that was never good enough for Southerners. It was actually disrespectful in their opinion. And they made it a point to make me aware of that quite regularly. I just didn't realize that me nodding in my typical urban fashion was a problem. That's what I was used to. It was rare that people would stop in Philly to actually speak. We just nodded. It was a city way of saying, 'Wassup'. The only time I remember everyone in Philly stopping to shake hands was right after the Million Man March. But eventually that was all forgotten about.

Aunt Rochelle and I walked into the financial aid building, but security wouldn't let us upstairs.

"I'm sorry, guys." said Bernie, a light skinned buff guy that my aunt made eyes at. He made some back at her, too. "I really can't let you up."

"Why not?" said Aunt Rochelle.

"There's a list. They're going strictly by that."

"How long is the list?"

"There's about a hundred people on there already. They're hoping to see everyone by five. But they're supposed to shut down at four."

"They're planning on shutting down at four o' clock and registration was an hour late? And this is the first day of school? They must be out of their cotton picking ever loving minds."

"Hey, I agree. People aren't happy."

115

"Well, look, Bernie, this is my nephew. We need to get up there."

"I really can't."

"I work here. I'm over at the Starks Building. Student Support. Right now I'm supporting my nephew. We need to get up there."

My aunt worked him hard. Batting the eyelashes, puckering the lips, smiling and speaking with a soft sexy drawl, and flexing the muscles of her derriere. His face was blushing pink as the lipstick on my aunt's lips. Lips that Bernie seemed to be fixated on when not looking at her um, *healthy* upper package. He opened the door slowly.

"Don't tell them I let you up." he said.

"We won't." I responded. "Thank you."

My aunt and I walked up a flight and into a small room. The office was filled with about twelve students. Some of them had their parents with them. Parents can make administrators lose their minds. That same intimidation crap some administrators try to scare students with, the parents will always have them beat. Especially moms. Real moms who love their children will fight so hard for them. Especially when moms are dealing with their sons. I'm a mama's boy, I admit it. I'm not the stereotypical mama's boy. But I'm a mama's boy nonetheless. And my mom and I have a friendship, not just a mother- son relationship. A true friendship. Mothers will kill for their children if they could. Mothers will stand in front of a bullet. Push them out of the way if a car's about to hit them, so they can get hit instead. Mothers can be in a position where they're weak, but thinking about their children gives them an unbreakable strength. And Aunt Rochelle had to put the fear of a mother into these folks.

The Office Administrator had absolutely no customer service skills whatsoever. And financial aid is a customer service type situation. We as students were being serviced. And we as students were taking out loans that we had to pay back. So technically we were customers. And that office was the manager of the funds that we were to receive. But this young lady who looked to be my age (I think she graduated here last year), had a crunched up face, poked out lips, and the way her body was hanging off her chair it was evident that her existence was misplaced. She started giving my aunt lip service about my stuff not being in order. She ignored that my mother and I got the thumbs up that everything was everything. And she nor her co-workers would dare admit to making a mistake. I knew that the volcano was erupting. My aunt was about to ooze lava. I hoped that she would keep her actions tranquil. I knew how she could get.

I remembered this one time when we were on I-95, there was a traffic jam because this guy in a convertible nearly hit us. Aunt Rochelle got out of her car in the middle of the stretch and started mouthing off at this dude. I was concerned. It was a frightening case of road rage. She already blew at people if they drove like nuts. And I totally sympathized with her, but people are liable to pull guns out of their glove compartments and blow your head off.

My aunt was a southern belle just like Mom-Mom. She'd only been living in Raleigh for about a decade or so. But she picked up every southern nuance one could think of. But in dealing with this young lady, my aunt had no choice but to reveal that she still had some Philly left in her. Aunt Rochelle told that woman off. She told her that they had to let me register. They had to let me move into my room. Even if I came back tomorrow or the next day to clear up the matter. She told her that I had nowhere else to go. I was stranded. She was lying. She wouldn't have left me on the street. But she wanted them to know that they had to take care of me. If it meant getting me a hotel room, then so be it. She never told them that we were related. She had her reasons. I couldn't blame her. She had a rep. Not necessarily a bad one. But a rep. A rep for being a strong black woman that didn't take any crap. She didn't believe in the cliquish behavior exhibited by her co-workers, by her boss, and by the administration. No, my aunt was real. 100% real.

And Aunt Rochelle loved and respected me so much that she didn't want people's perceptions of me to be dictated by people's perceptions of her. The administration didn't like her too much. She challenged them. Not because she wanted a fight. But she didn't have a choice. It was much like self-defense. If someone comes at you with rolling fists, you can run off to seek safety and shelter. You can stand there and allow yourself to be beat with no aversion. Or you can fight either physically or mentally. All the folks who had some hand in raising me, were ingredients that were cooked to make me into the man that I became. My mother gave me the morals and values. My grandmother was my spirit. My grandfather was my example. My Aunt Vanessa was my voice of reason. My Aunt Rochelle was my boxing coach. I guess I watched her in the ring. Because it turned out that I'd have to step in there myself quite often.

# CHAPTER 19

# "SUPERHERO & SHOW TUNE SCENARIOS"

I WENT THROUGH THREE room mates at Readmore College. I didn't enjoy either of the experiences. Some have said that perhaps my room mates weren't the problem. Maybe I was. I disagree. I'm not that difficult to get along with. I'm actually one of the nicest people you'd ever meet. I find it hard to tell people 'No'. I may not always smile, but it's not because I'm upset. I just have a tendency to wear my emotion on my face. And my emotion is typically one of concern over my future. I'm always thinking about it. I'm always dreaming. And brainstorming ways to make those dreams no longer be dreams anymore. That indifferent pose of my cheekbones and the veins on my forehead were just my aspirations speaking to my soul.

I wasn't hard to chill with. But I expected intelligence from everyone.

I only moved in a few of my belongings to my room. I felt apprehensive to add any more because the room was riddled with mutant cockroaches. They were five times the normal size. And some of them had wings. And they'd crawl out from underneath the beds and closets. And sit above me on the ceilings staring down at me like a hawk. Always at odd times. They were never around when I just happened to be standing or sitting there. They always crept when they thought we weren't paying attention. I'd be asleep in bed, and be awakened by my mentally challenged biological timepiece. I'd roll over in bed and there the roaches were having a good ol' time. And sometimes they even had visitors, little gray things with tails. And the room was dark. Only the moonlight reflected into this environment. And it was cold. And though the building had other residents, I felt lonely and isolated. Perhaps due in part to my being a new face in this place. Yet still, I felt unaccompanied at all times.

I didn't stay in the room much. Maybe three or four times the whole semester. Aunt Rochelle lived nearby. I couldn't resist being there in a place where I could watch television into the wee hours of the morning. A place where I could urinate and groom freely. A place where I didn't have to adhere to the rules of the school. And unlike my semi-stressful times with my aunt and her son back in junior high, I was now more mature. I was able to handle her. She was able to handle me. Still,

I felt guilty most of the time. I was dependent on her to get where I needed to get. I still wasn't driving. And I knew that I was getting on her nerves. She wouldn't admit it directly. But she hinted, saying things like: 'You really need to experience campus life'. I understood that I was busting her groove. But I hardly needed to experience campus life. Been there, done that. Not fun. Not for me. Plenty of folks I knew enjoyed the campus life to the max. But I've pretty much always been a rather monotonous person. The parties and dances were never my scene. Watching a movie or reading a good book was my night of clubbing.

One Friday, my aunt kicked me out. She told me that I had to stay on campus because she was having some of her girls over for a ladies night. Her son was staying with a friend of his in Cary. I packed an overnight bag and went over to my room. It was then that I discovered it was no longer my room. My refrigerator, microwave, and television had been expunged. And sleeping on my sheets was someone else. Because I hadn't slept in my room in some time, the housing representatives assumed that I was no longer boarding. Yet they were still taking my money. They didn't even check to see if I was alive and well. What was the point of me signing all that paperwork, which included putting down several emergency names and contacts? I could have been dead in a creek somewhere for all they knew. They didn't even have the common courtesy to call and ask if I was planning on leaving my half of the room vacant.

My aunt was livid at the matter. Not really because she wanted her privacy. But more so because my stuff was missing and we didn't know where. It turned out that housing sold my belongings to another student. Was that even legal? My aunt told those people off. And that was after I said what I had to say. It took some time, but I eventually was repaid one hundred and fifty dollars for my losses. It wasn't nearly as much as it should have been. That only paid for the cost of my fridge. But at least someone was finally taking responsibility for something they did. Needless to say, I didn't jump at the chance for them to kick the new guy out so I could move back in. I couldn't get off the meal plan because the semester was paid for. I never ate in the cafeteria. The food was less than desirable. Not that I blamed anyone about that. I realized they had many mouths to feed and that many mouths had certain dietary restrictions. It was clear to see why one had to douse their meals in salt and pepper. I went back to my aunt's. Much to her concealed chagrin.

The following semester, I had no choice but to stay on campus. My aunt finally made it mandatory. Every morning my alarm clock was the sound of the 'Power Rangers'. I had no problem with the show itself. That used to be my favorite. But that was when I was a kid. My new room mate seemed to be addicted. And he'd blast it every morning at 6am. And if it wasn't that blaring loudly from the TV set, it was wrestling. And if it wasn't wrestling, it was a video game. And video games were the worst. He played them all the time. All the time! And he even had a nerve to place signs all around the dorm advertising our room as 'The Game Room'. It's no wonder why our room was always crawling with folks. And people had the audacity to sit on my bed while they socialized. I don't play when it comes to that. My bed is my refuge. My bed is my temple. My bed is mine. I had to literally rope off my bed with electrical tape and posters. I'm sure some people probably sat on it just because they thought I was being a prick. But don't touch what's not yours. That's how I feel. And my room mate seemed not to care if I was watching my TV first. He would still turn up the volume on his set. And he was a loud person. His voice was like a megaphone.

I really didn't take the time to get to know him. I was rather repulsed by his behavior. I was already stressed out because registration had lost all my information again. And my pre-registration had somehow been deleted from the system. My room mate seemed kindhearted, but also inconsiderate. I shouldn't have had to spell it out for him. It's called common courtesy. And he just didn't have it. He was a freshman. And the freshman mentality was ingrained in his personality. This had to have been his first time away from home. And he lived only a few hours away. It's not like he was in a different world. But then I guess college is a different world. Hence the name of the sitcom from back in the day. He seemed like that bag of popcorn that sat in that old, old microwave that was moving too slow. And then finally he was able to POP-POP-POP. But I hated being splashed with his salt and butter. I was chastised by many for not properly dealing with the situation. Rather than confront him about his actions, I put in a request for a room change.

I understood others' opinions. Truly I did. But I also knew that it would have been easier said than done, to be civil with him if I had confronted him. I wouldn't have used my hands, but my words I'm certain would have been painstakingly arctic. I didn't want a battle with him. I didn't know him. He didn't know me. But I was heated. Very heated. And the last time I was real heated with a room mate, I was almost kicked out for speaking my mind. I wasn't afraid to speak my mind in this situation. But I was already falling victim to the abrasions of academia and administrative war. After going down the short list of candidates for my new room mate, I stopped when I came across a name that I knew. Slightly knew. I didn't know him. But I had seen him in passing. And I was aware that he was in my major. We both were Film, Theatre, and Media Arts (FTM) majors. His name was Saffron Jackson. He even had a showbiz name. I was sure that I had finally found the greatest room mate of all time. Finally!

The Dean of Housing informed Saffron on Tuesday that I'd be moving in on Thursday. But when Thursday came, all of his stuff was still strewn about. I left note after note for the next few days. And still he had not removed anything. It wasn't until Tuesday of the following week when housing bit his ear about the situation, that he finally made a place for me. Already things seemed to be getting off to a rocky beginning. He was a dark skinned diminutive chap with straight hair and a freckled face. The first thing he did was sit down on his bed and face me, his eyes staring at me like that of a puppy who has misplaced his bone.

"Are you clean?" he asked me without hesitation.

"Pardon?" I replied, completely confused by his inquest.

"Are you clean?"

"Yes, I'm clean."

"Good. Very good. Because I'm clean and I like to keep things clean. As clean as possible. It's very important to me."

I didn't know what to say after that. It was such a direct way of asking such a question. I wasn't sure why he even asked. But I looked around the room and saw that it was indeed uncontaminated by the toxic pollutants of the world. He reminded me so much of my aunt. He seemed very anal about the placement of his belongings throughout the room. Whenever I accidentally bumped into his desk and knocked one of his flag statues to the floor, he'd come back and have a bloody fit that their positions had changed. I tried to be meticulous about putting things exactly where they were previously. But obviously, I was unsuccessful. Saffron may have been riled because the flags meant something to him. He wore dog tags around his neck. His father was a military man. But as much as he talked about his family, and I don't mean in a good way, it's hard to believe that because of his father he has allegiance for the flag.

Whenever Saffron's mother called, he would say: 'What does that bitch want?'. He often mumbled to people how completely screwed up his family was. He said that his mother was having an affair, or multiple affairs to be more accurate. And he always used the 'b' word or something worse to describe her. And he didn't seem all too happy with his father either. He hated the fact they had to travel so much during his childhood. This probably contributed to him finding it hard to make friends with people. But he was more standoffish than I was. He wasn't very friendly. He wasn't mean either. He was undefined. I just couldn't understand how he could hate his mother so much. A person would have to hate their mother to call her that name. That's the worst name any man could ever call a woman. But when that woman is his mother, the woman who carried him in her womb for nine months, it's irrevocable.

Saffron was also more inconsiderate than my last room mate. He had no respect whatsoever. He told me that to get respect, I'd have to earn it. How could I not have earned it? I was nothing but sincere and thoughtful. I was hoping that he and I would be able to collaborate at some point. And since I was an upperclassman, I figured that perhaps he'd be interested in me showing him what I knew. And I'd be more than happy to learn from him, too. A true artist never stops learning. I don't care if it's Tom Cruise or Denzel Washington. Any true artist that says they know it all may not be as true as they profess. The process never reaches conclusion. It just goes on and on and on. But this guy thought I was Satan. Some friends told me that he was probably jealous or envious. I saw how that could be a possibility. And it was probably a mixture of both. I have this theory that jealousy and envy are two different animals. That jealousy is unhealthy. But envy is merely admiration. Don't ask me why my mind thinks like that. But that's what I came up with at the time, and it seems to have stuck.

I think Saffron hated me or something. I had done a lot, but I wasn't pompous about it. Plenty of people thought I was though. But if that's how I came off, it was purely unintentional. For every project I did, I was the last person that mattered. I always made sure that my cast and crew received as much if not more attention than myself. And when we did press interviews and stuff, I had to direct them to speak because I refused to be a microphone hog. I couldn't pay them. All I could do was give them some extra experience to put in their dossier. This guy went so far as to put up posters on his wall with various quotes. I don't even recall what the quotes said, or who said them. But they were strong quotes that talked about how he was already on the route to fame. And how I was an enemy but he needed to keep me close. Stuff like that. And keeping me close was something I couldn't control. I was trapped in a room with him. And things would be this way for the next four months. And he loved that he had a certain hold over me. I tried not to let my feelings show, but he tested me every chance he got.

We weren't allowed to have microwaves or space heaters that semester because the dorm's electrical system was not up to code. Sparks frequently jumped out of the sockets. And the air and heating system there had minds of their own. When the outside temp was cold, the air inside was on full blast. And vice-versa. I refused to freeze my butt off. I took some cardboard and placed it over our vents. He had a raging fit and cussed me out. He didn't like the fact I put cardboard over his vent. I suppose I should have asked him first. But he wasn't even around at the time I needed to do it. He just stormed into the room, grabbed a chair, stood on it, and yanked the cardboard down like a madman. He then ripped it up and dropped it into my trash can. He really expected me to sit around all semester wearing a hat, scarf, and gloves. I did it for one weekend while trying to prepare for midterms. But I refused to keep doing it. I was paying thousands just like him to be in that room. I kept housing abreast of the situation on a daily basis. He accused me of being a tattle-tale. Maybe I was. But I needed a little bit of comfort. I never expected college to be 100% stress free. But this stress was unnecessary. I can't help it if someone wishes not to be civil with me. He was the one who said he didn't understand why people made such a big deal about air conditioners. He said if people were hot then they should open a window. Why couldn't he take his own advice?

I opened the window one day and re-covered the vents. He began yelling to the top of his lungs. It was finally happening. A sequel to my shouting match with Kenny Jung. Only this time, I really was seconds away from aiming my fist. I sat on my bed very still, but clinching my teeth. And clinching my fists. Slowly boiling. Saffron was pacing back and forth with demonic possession. Calling me every name in the Dictionary of the Profane. His face flushed in fiery orange. I called a friend of mine down on the first floor, and warned him that he may want to come upstairs and try to help iron things out, before I did something I may regret. He told me to sit tight and he'd be up in a few minutes. I didn't know if a few minutes was enough time. One of us might be hurt in that time. This moment was the breaking point for me.

I didn't make a big deal when he watched show tunes and musicals on his TV. Even though he had them blasted loud. Even though most of the time, I was trying to watch my TV, which I had turned on first. Even though he had an earphone jack on his TV set and I didn't. I didn't make a big deal. I didn't make a big deal that he had to perform every single scene from 'The Color Purple' and 'Moulin Rouge' every day and every night. Word for frigging word! I didn't make a big deal. I even managed to ignore him as best I could when he'd turn up his radio late at night to try and drown out mine. I admit that sometimes I didn't have a choice but to give an eye for an eye and turn mine up, too. But usually, I pretended he didn't exist. He got off on me responding to his antics. He thought it was funny. I didn't complain when he shouted words of blasphemy and dissed the bible, complaining that much of it was questionable. And when he professed he wasn't sure he believed in God. Even if his concerns had validity, I wasn't interested in hearing them. But I didn't complain.

Sometimes it isn't meant for two people to be in the same room. Sometimes one of those people has to learn. And grow up. And burn their finger on the stove a few times to get the message that the stove is hot. And sometimes one of those people is destined to be to themselves. Not lonely, not alone. Just to themselves. That was the case with Saffron and I. You can decipher which group belongs to whom. That experience taught me that the grass isn't always greener on the other side. I ended up having a few classes with the 'Power Rangers' kid the following semester. And I discovered that he was a gifted artist. Had the voice of a songbird. And he was cool. Funny, crazy, and cool. Perhaps fate didn't have it in the cards for us to be successful room mates, but I was happy that I received another chance to associate with him. Even if we were to never see or speak again. It would have hurt me personally to leave a place, knowing that most of the relationships I was a part of left a bad taste in my mouth. It was good to know that one of my room mates wasn't an unlikable person. And it was good to know that there was one bridge that perhaps I didn't burn.

The final semester of school was a banner one for me. It was the year that I refused to be in a room with anyone. I told the Provost and Vice President of Readmore that me living with someone else was not an option. That I was entitled to a room by myself. I had made the grade. I made all of the honors' lists. Even President's List. And I was a graduating senior. I deserved to get a break. I was charged a five hundred dollar private room fee. Though I was displeased with having to pay for some extra solace since it seemed like the school was mooching off of every dime I had, or didn't have, I gave in. I gave in because I knew that in order for my final semester to be one that I could be proud of, I needed time to myself. And I knew that since all my classes would be general education requirements, I needed no distractions. I wish that my last semester had only been classes in the arts. But the FTM Director strongly suggested upon my arrival two and a half years ago that I take all the classes in my major because they were only offered at certain times.

CHAPTER 20

# "IN THIS CORNER…"

WHEN I ARRIVED AT Readmore, I was so happy to learn that they had a bona fide, state of the art theatre and film program. I would be using equipment that the big boys were using. After years of being deceived (intentionally or not), I was finally in where I belonged. My first act of duty was meeting with the Director of FTM. His name was Jeffrey Berkwowitz. He was a small emaciated Jewish man with too-thick framed spectacles. He sat behind his desk in a small office on the North side of campus. His walls were made of concrete and his windows were tinted. This kept some of the sunlight out. Already I was feeling something in my gut. But I ignored it. He claimed he didn't know that I'd be enrolling so soon. Yet he had been courting me during my entire season working on the TV show back home. I gave him the benefit of a doubt. He probably had a lot of work and a lot of names to deal with. So remembering me probably wasn't possible. But then I later found out that only ten students were in this department. Not to mention, I'm sure that my portfolio outdid everyone else's. It turned out that there really were no other portfolios to outshine. My mother enclosed my portfolio as backup information with the application. It wasn't something that the college requested. So none of the other students in the program had to submit portfolios. And it wouldn't have mattered because none of them had any to submit anyway.

I asked Mr. Berkowitz if I could see some of the work he produced. If I was to be taught by someone, I wanted to peruse their credentials. The same way they perused mine. I wanted to know if he indeed was an expert. I couldn't find any information on the Internet about him. And here at the school he was the Artist In Residence. So where was his art? He quickly changed subjects. I then asked to see some of the projects produced by previous classes. The arts program was only five years old that semester, and I was anxious to see how it had evolved since its inception. But it seemed as if he was reluctant to release any of those things. I wasn't sure why. But he evaded any questions I had relating to his work, or the work of his students. He either changed topics or took sips of the coffee on his desk. Or fiddled with file folders. Or pressed buttons on his phone. Or keys on his computer keypad. What was it that he didn't want me to know? I wondered. But only for a moment. Then I let it go.

I was impressed with the equipment at my disposal. Digital Video Cameras, editing systems, a soundstage (a mini-soundstage), an actual theatre. Not everything was as up to date as Mr. Berkowitz made things sound whenever he discussed the program in a public forum. But I didn't let it bother me because the blank page stared at me, and I was inspired to put something on it. I was intent on using all that to my advantage. And trust me, I did. I probably spent more time in the school's Edit Lab than anyone else.

Mr. Jalen was the Associate Professor of Film. He was a white guy with a long ponytail that went to the top of his backside. He was young. In his late twenties probably. Fresh out of graduate school. And he wasn't just a teacher. He was an artist. A struggling artist. But not a disgruntled one. There's a major difference between the two. He was cool. Cool and real. And he spoke to us all like we were on his level. Not like a teacher to his pupil. Or a father to his son. And I appreciated that. He told me that he could instantly tell that I might be in the wrong place. At first, I wasn't sure what to make of that. I stood in front of him, silent. Standing in Room C132, home of Dramatic Structure I. He invited me out to Bojangles, a fast-food joint up the street.

While eating a chicken meal in a booth, Mr. Jalen was very frank with me.

"I'm gonna cut straight to the point, man." he said, "You're talented. You might even be too talented to be around here. As a professor here, I'm really not allowed to tell you to leave Readmore. But I think you're a bright guy. And I'm not sure if you're gonna get what you want out of this place. All I'm saying is, if you think you might be planning to head off to another school, now would be the time. The longer you wait the more chance you have of credits not transferring, and you being pigeonholed here. I know you're going places, and I wish you the best of luck."

It was a very kind thing for him to have a heart to heart talk with me. While not all the pieces of the puzzle seemed to fit snugly, I was leery about relocating for a third time. I wanted to finish and finally be finished. And here, I was at least body-guarded by my aunt. And I didn't know it then, but the pep talk and goodbye speech that Mr. Jalen gave me really wasn't for me. Or if it was, he must have realized in speaking to me, that maybe he needed to practice what he preached. Because it wasn't too long before I learned that he would not be returning the following semester. There were rumors that his fiancée had received a job offer in Atlanta. There were rumors that he received a job offer at a community college there, too. I was never sure what his actual reason for leaving was. But I saw firsthand that his crumbling civility with Mr. Berkowitz was tearing him apart. One afternoon, I happened to be passing by the stairwell and I heard loud shouting voices. I crept over to the door and cracked it open just a few inches. It was then and there that I saw the two film instructors verbally fist fighting. It had something to do with them disagreeing on a major curriculum change for the next academic cycle. But it also had something to do with Mr. Berkowitz's attitude.

The FTM Director thought he was hot stuff. And that someone was supposed to treat him like a king. He was arrogant. And he always boasted about how many films he produced, screenplays he wrote, and celebrities he had affiliation with. Yet none of those celebrities ever came to talk to us about their experiences in the business. We never saw any of his films. And an occasional glance at one of his four page scripts for class was not satisfactory. He played urban films in class because as he put it, 'I'm sure you guys can relate to this." We could relate to it because we were black? And when he took students that he deemed, and these are his words: 'worthy', to a film festival in New York City, we felt ridiculed. At least I did. He openly said on panel discussions in front of predominately white audiences that he was happy to introduce us to new experiences and fancy restaurants. He didn't know a thing about me. I was probably more cultured than he was. And that café we ate at that morning was far from posh. And speaking of eating, he said in front of other professors that accompanied us, and establishment patrons, that he was glad to see us learning how to balance our checks. I may not have been John Nash, but balancing my checks had never been a problem for me.

At the festival, Mr. Berkowitz chose a short film by one of my peers, Evan, to screen for the audience. He told them that Evan was trying to find himself through the making of his motion picture comedy. It seemed like this instructor was merely trying to save another little Negro boy. No offense to Evan's film. I thought it had a lot of promise. But it featured the stereotypical images of young black men who were playas, trying to score some sex with as many virgins as possible. There seemingly wasn't a message. Just a funny piece with funny characters and funny lines. Not everything has to be dramatically intense. But for Mr. Berkowitz to have this particular project be the flagship of our entire program was reprehensible. Was this really the image he wanted to portray of the young filmmakers and artists at Readmore? Didn't he want us to be as good as, if not better than the mainstream college and university students? If everyone just thinks that we're a bunch of inner city black kids that he's trying to save by introducing us to film, that's great for him, but it sucks for us. Because it isn't true. I've known my calling for years. He didn't make me an artist. I made myself an artist.

And I didn't have a problem being taught filmmaking by white and Jewish instructors. But each time they tried to cater certain classes to the struggle of the minority filmmaker, I was forced to reevaluate my respect level for them. For Berkowitz. And Ms. Blake, the new Associate Professor of Film, and the Theatre Director, Mr. Ryan. They never even arranged it so that we could visit film sets on a regular basis that had a strong minority presence. They didn't facilitate workshops or guest lectures in which the panelists or speakers were minorities. It didn't matter if they were Black, Asian, Latino or Female. We got nothing.

When I revealed my concerns to the Provost and Vice-President, he claimed that announcements for campus positions were put out, but no minorities qualified. I didn't believe a word that came from his lips. Where were the announcements being placed? In what newspapers? Were any put in the minority based publications of North Carolina? Were any sent to other schools, businesses, and workplaces? Were announcements sent to other states and cities? Something seemed fishy to me. I was a black man. At a black college. In the arts major. Being taught by no blacks. I refused to keep quiet about that. And let's just say that everyone was well aware of how I felt. Some tried to deny it, but they knew. And even if I hadn't voiced my concern, didn't these folks get a college education themselves? Seems to me that their own intelligence should have opened their eyes to the world around them. They were working at a black school, with black kids who needed a black influence every now and then. Part of receiving the black college experience is supposed to be increasing one's knowledge of their culture. And sometimes our culture was as simple as the folks we brushed shoulders with. They were our culture. We were our culture. Readmore College was our culture.

## CHAPTER 21

———◆◆◆◆———

# "I'LL NEVER FORGET"

THANK GOD THE DAYS are finally winding down. They say you can't wait for the day to leave college, but when you leave it, you'll miss it. I'm not sure if I will or not. But I know that I'll miss some of the friendships I've made with some students. And even with some of the staff and faculty. I'll never forget those whom I can actually call 'friend'. They helped me get through what I considered to be tough times. Even if all they did was put a smile on my face for five minutes. Or put a hand on my shoulder for a few moments. Or simply offer a smile in passing. Or do an unexpected good deed for me. Or give a buck here and there if I was low on funds. That's what I'll miss. Many things I saw while schooling. Many things I said. Many things I didn't say. Many things I did. Many things I didn't. But regardless, I'll never forget.

I'll never forget the young men who drove onto campus blaring loud profane music from their car speakers as they passed the security booth and the Administration Building, which housed the Office of The President. I'll never forget Parlor Hall. This dormitory was nicknamed 'The Projects' of the campus. The five story residence was where they usually put all the Freshmen and the students who weren't exactly making the grade. Trash was always all over the lawns. Emptied bottles and cans of alcoholic beverage, used condoms, condom wrappers and other garbage. Whenever the weather agreed the place was usually crawling with what looked like society's degenerates. Young ladies dressed in mini-skirts, tank tops, and stockings. Parading back and forth like it was a hooker strip. Too much makeup on, bright colors, etc. And young men dressed like hoods, discreetly or not so discreetly, passing items from hand to hand. Drug deals. And all this happened right across the lawn from security. Maybe security knew what was going on. Maybe they were a part of it. I guess I'll never know for sure.

I'll never forget the jocks who made liars out of everyone who said that: 'all jocks are stupid and *play* instead of *pay* for their college education'. I'll never forget the jocks who couldn't read and write, but were allowed to slip through the collegiate cracks because administration wanted to look good, come game time. I'll never forget how administration supported building sports facilities on campus, but never explained why there was hardly any toilet tissue, or paper towels in the bathroom. And why it seemed that the other majors within the school seemed to take a backseat to football, basketball and golf. And why administration never came to our school shows and arts presentations. And why administration said: 'Hello' or 'Good morning' to us when they felt the urge to. I'll never forget the administration who always made themselves available for students to talk. And the administration whose door seemed to always be shut. I'll never forget how administration seemed more concerned with recruiting new students, instead of embracing the ones they already had. And how administration casually swept internal embezzlement scandals right on under the rug.

I'll never forget the late night and early morning fire drills. I'll never forget the times my peers mischievously pulled the fire alarms. I'll never forget the time my dorm was raided. And forty something girls were taken out of the dorm because they were underage. And large amounts of narcotics were confiscated. And how it seemed that nearly everyone was in bed with someone else. I'll never forget my peers who spit and urinated in the hallways and stairwells. I'll never forget my peers who put catsup all over the buttons on the elevator console. I'll never forget my peers who stole my towels and clothes off the hook while I was showering. I'll never forget my peers who left their droppings all over the toilet seats and surrounding areas. I'll never forget the vermin that slept on the toilet tissue rolls. I'll never forget my peers who threw water bottles and water balloons out of five story windows at unsuspecting passers-by. I'll never forget the peers who smeared others' reps by scribbling their names, numbers and defamatory remarks on bathroom and elevator walls. I'll never forget the peers who thought being eternally intoxicated was cute.

I'll never forget the innocent young men who were caught in the wrong place at the wrong time. And how they were incarcerated for crimes they did not commit. And how Readmore did not support them, or try to find the truth. How this school allowed these students' names and reputations to be slandered, and their lives and educational lives to be destroyed. How even when some of them returned after miraculously being acquitted, or dismissed criminally, there was no welcoming back with open arms. I'll never forget my brothas who went to lockup for whatever reason and came back to school a Muslim on a mission. I'll never forget the ones who came back from lockup with a false idea of what the Muslim religion was. The ones who grew their hair all out of place, wore the long garb and preached the gospel, not really getting what it was all about and what they were really doing. I'm not Muslim, but it doesn't take a genius to recognize that there's a difference. You've got the truly reformed 100% bona fide Muslim. And then you've got the 100% bona fide *prison Muslim* who claims to be wise, but in truth knows squat.

I'll never forget my peers who spurted the 'N' word at each other because they felt that if they used the term affectionately, it would take away the derogative meaning of the word. I'll never forget how most of them failed to even see that it shouldn't matter. That it's the principle of the thing. That we shouldn't be saying it to each other period. The same way that Asians shouldn't call each other Slant Eyes or Chinks. The same way that Whites shouldn't call themselves Honky or Cracker. The same way that other races shouldn't call Hispanics Ese. The same way that Jews shouldn't call each other Nickel-Nose. That the word 'nigger' (or 'nigga', 'nigguh', and/or 'nig') really means ignorant. And that if that's the way we view each other, then maybe we all really are just a bunch of 'niggers'.

I'll never forget my peers who'd rather have bloodshot eyes from smoking pot and black lips from doing acid instead of going to class. And the ones who went to class, but were still high as a kite. Just smiling silly or looking zombied. I'll never forget the teachers and administrators who attempted, and/or succeeded at crossing the line with students.

I'll never forget my peers who found it acceptable to come out of the house (and dorm), looking a hot mess. The ones who didn't understand one should always be dressed for success, as one never knows who one might encounter. It may be one's future boss. Or a police officer who decides to give one a warning instead of a ticket or slap on the wrists, solely because of the clothes one is wearing. None of us should be judged on how we look. But let's face it, we have all made assumptions. We assume that the guy with a Mohawk and all black is a Goth kid. We assume the girl with a see-thru top is a prostitute. We assume the guy with a grill in his mouth and a jersey on his back, is the black man that robbed the Five and Dime on Wadsworth. We assume that the overweight girl who doesn't wear makeup is a lesbian. We assume that the kid who doesn't like to brag about sexually related topics is gay.

I'll never forget the young women who left college for the summer, thin, and returned with buns in the oven. I'll never forget the young women who were abused next door to me. How their boyfriends slammed them into the wall so hard, items on my shelf rattled. How one was threatened to be thrown out of the window. How when I called security, they arrived too late. I'll never forget witnessing drug deals go down right across the hall. Room 200 was a pharmacy for sure. I'll never forget the young men who were such pretty boys that it made the ladies swoon. I'll never forget how some of these men were 'The seducers' and some were 'The seduced'. I'll never forget the young ladies who couldn't say 'No'. And the ones who said 'No', but were ignored.

I'll never forget the good times. I'll never forget the bad times. And I'll never forget the times in between.

—◆✕◆—

# CHAPTER 22

# "LAST LOOKS"

EVEN THOUGH THE SUN was smiling, her warmth wasn't nearly as strong as usual. There was a breeze and it wouldn't go away. Mom-Mom was in the kitchen ironing my gown and sash. My aunts were snapping photographs. And my mother was in the bathroom giving herself last looks and final touches. I was sitting on the couch occasionally glancing at a photograph. The person in the photograph was the missing link. The day was promising, yet bittersweet. We were without my grandfather. Pop-Pop had tragically succumbed to a heart attack or two, several months prior. I wasn't letting his absence downplay the excitement that was brewing. I felt it my responsibility to go on with that day as if he were there. Because in a sense, he was. In my heart. In our hearts.

I didn't want my family to be sad. It was a special day. Not only for me, but for everyone. It was the day that I'd be recognized for my diligent scholarship. My graduation. Aunt Rochelle was already misty-eyed because she had always looked forward to Pop-Pop being able to smile proudly when his grandson walked across the stage to receive his degree. But he was smiling proud from wherever he was. That I knew. I think my family still assumed that Pop-Pop was the source of my meditation. But my melancholy mood wasn't that at all. It was just subdued enthusiasm. I may not have been bouncing off walls. But I felt like my opportunity to breathe again was on the horizon. It had been a long time coming. Because I did work hard, I deserved all the riches life had to offer. Not necessarily financial riches, but the riches that real life would bring.

I was never exactly a walking commercial for my soon to be alma mater. And everyone knew it. And it really tampered with the elastic of my domestic relationships. But it didn't take long for me to differentiate between the school and the administration. I never hated the school, contrary to others' beliefs. Readmore had a rich history and unfortunately it was never revealed by administrative sources what that history entailed. Were it not for selected faculty, personal reading and research, and conversation with peers who actually found it lucrative to be knowledgeable; I'd be clueless to this day about what my historically black college had to offer. And what it had to offer was paramount.

Many of the negative situations and negative people actually taught me life lessons. So I appreciate the struggle. Because if the struggle ceased to exist, we'd never have dreams that we'd fight so vigorously to attain. And beyond that, I'd be selfish to think I was here on earth for any other reason than the fact something far greater than I, put me here. And that same force has had a plan for me since day one of my existence. And it's evident that any plan I desire will likely be overruled by the force's plan. This force has always spoken to me. I haven't always been obedient. But I know now that despite how cliché it may sound, things do occur for a reason. And while these reasons may not always be lucid to us, there are some things in life that are meant to remain a mystery. We can forever speculate. We can forever hate. We can forever be confused. We can forever try to destroy. But we didn't create this world, nor did we create ourselves. And regardless of what entity one believes in, one must believe in something greater than oneself. If one doesn't, one is kidding oneself.

A black man without a Diploma, and/or a Degree in America, is a recipe for disaster. There are some people who honestly can't obtain one. Some have had to take care of their families while also dealing with poverty and new age depression. Some are dying from incurable diseases. Some can't afford it. Some are homeless. Some are afraid. Some don't care. But the reality is, people look at you differently when you have a higher education. Especially when you're a minority. The masses already believe that we're ignorant fools.

And though we shouldn't have to, we have to prove them wrong. While any job is honorable, we're more than just maids and servants. We're just as good if not better than our racial counterparts. A simple piece of paper (the degree), says that you've mastered something. It says that you've accomplished something. It says that you're on your way to accomplishing something even bigger. And while everybody and I do mean everybody is somebody, the piece of paper that I not so long ago removed from the hand of the Readmore College President, will validate what has always been fact. I am somebody! Not everyone realizes that they're somebody. And in many cases it may just take receiving a degree for that realization to occur.

It really wouldn't have mattered what college I graduated from. Whether it was my first taste of black college life. Or my stab at white college life. Or my collegiate culmination. The main thing was that I did it. I made it through college. But being at an historically black institution, I was able to have many things happen that I shall never forget. I was able to touch the lives of others. I was able to inspire. I was able to encourage. And my life was able to be touched by others. And I was inspired. And I was encouraged. And I met people from all different walks of life. I met folks who on the outside seemed like the scum of the earth, but when I got to really know them, turned out to be individuals who might just change the world one day, and one step at a time. I met mothers finally receiving their higher education, while holding down various jobs to pay for loans. And I saw their sleep deprivation, and their tears, and their passion, and commitment to academic excellence. And every time I started to say things were tough for me, I'd think of them.

I witnessed the various struggles of my peers. Folks that really wanted to be in school, but ran out of money. Folks that were trying to make the grade yet were dealing with personal tragedies that cruelly tested them. Teachers and staff who didn't like the way things were going and tried to help us as best they could. And a whole lot more. And all this I was able to experience amongst my people. The minority population. I wish that some things were easier. And I wish that some things had been more challenging. But I can honestly say that I don't regret my HBCU experience for anything in the world. I'm stronger because of it. I'm a better fighter because of it. I'm a better listener because of it. I'm a better person because of it. All I pray is that future administrations at educational institutions worldwide understand what it is that we need, want, and should have. I pray that they understand what it means to be someone that we look up to.

They say when life gives you lemons, you make lemonade. But my HBCU experience wasn't a lemon. It was merely lemonade that needed to be sweetened. And between myself, and the friends I made there, we were the sugar.

## __THE END__

Printed in the United States
78369LV00001B/28-36